BRITAIN'S BIGGEST STAR

IS DAD?

D0494189

IVOR BADDIEL

SCHOLASTIC

Published in the UK by Scholastic Children's Books, 2021
Euston House, 24 Eversholt Street, London, NW1 1DB, UK
A division of Scholastic Limited.

London – New York – Toronto – Sydney – Auckland
Mexico City – New Delhi – Hong Kong

SCHOLASTIC and associated logos are trademarks and/or
registered trademarks of Scholastic Inc.

Text © Ivor Baddiel, 2021
Illustrations © James Lancett, 2021

The right of Ivor Baddiel to be identified as the author
of this work has been asserted by him under the
Copyright, Designs and Patents Act 1988.

ISBN 978 0702 30058 5

A CIP catalogue record for this book is available
from the British Library.

All rights reserved.
This book is sold subject to the condition that it shall not,
by way of trade or otherwise, be lent, hired out or otherwise
circulated in any form of binding or cover other than that in which
it is published. No part of this publication may be reproduced, stored
in a retrieval system, or transmitted in any form or by any means
(electronic, mechanical, photocopying, recording or otherwise)
without prior written permission of Scholastic Limited.

Printed by CPI Group (UK) Ltd, Croydon, CR0 4YY
Papers used by Scholastic Children's Books are made
from wood grown in sustainable forests.

1 3 5 7 9 10 8 6 4 2

This is a work of fiction. Names, characters, places, incidents
and dialogues are products of the author's imagination or are used
fictitiously. Any resemblance to actual people, living or dead,
events or locales is entirely coincidental.

www.scholastic.co.uk

To Colleen, The Father. A Huge Star.

DUDLEY LIBRARIES	
000003080519	
Askews & Holts	19-Apr-2021
JF S	£6.99
2ST	

CHAPTER 1

Not So Secret Agent

"Please don't tell anyone you've seen me. Please, please, please, pleaaaaaaaasssssssseeeeee!"

Now this was awkward. With a capital A, followed by a capital W-K-W-A-R-D. That's how awkward it was.

Rewind a bit, though. . .

"!Eeeeessssssssaaaaaaaaelp, esaelp, esaelp, esaelp. Em nees ev'uoy enoyna llet t'nod esaelp."

. . .and there was no awkwardness. It was just a normal day for thirteen-year-old twins Harry and Abby Moore.

They were walking home from an ordinary day at school – so ordinary, in fact, that it might have gone down in history as The Most Ordinary Day of All Time, though of course that would have made it not so ordinary – when Harry suggested that they take a different route back.

Harry suggested this regularly, almost every day, and it had very little to do with him actually wanting to go home a different way and a lot to do with him wanting to annoy Abby.

Annoying Abby was one of Harry's favourite pastimes, something he was particularly good at and had been working on since the day they were born. (It infuriated her that technically he was older – by a whole eight minutes.)

He also liked annoying Abby because it was so easy.

Harry and Abby were not just "non-identical" twins, they were "non-identical in every way, shape or form" twins.

Abby was tall, with straight hair and brown eyes, whilst Harry was shorter, with curly hair and grey-green eyes. In fact, the usual reaction when they told people they were twins was a snort and a look which said, *Do you really think I'm that stupid?*, a question which Harry or Abby generally thought it best not to answer.

As for their personalities, well, chalk and cheese had more in common. Abby was practical and organized. When she did the washing-up, she always did it in an orderly fashion, stacking the items according to size and shape, and transferring them to the cupboard once they were dry, quickly and efficiently.

Harry had a far more carefree and creative approach to life. He was always looking for ways to make the washing-up different and entertaining, such as doing it blindfolded or with one hand (neither went well).

So when it came to walking home from school, Abby saw no reason not to take the most direct route, *every single day*.

This, of course, gave Harry ample opportunity to annoy her.

"Hey, let's go through the park," he said. "I think there's a wormhole under the see-saw in the playground."

Abby sighed. "Why," she said, "would there be a wormhole under the see-saw in the playground?"

"Naresh read this book about them and he says they can pop up where there are fluctuations in the atmosphere," said Harry. "So it makes sense that there'd be one under a see-saw. And if there *is* a wormhole there, it will get us home much sooner."

"The only hole I'm interested in is your cakehole, and in particular, shutting it," Abby said.

"Fine," said Harry. "Go your boring old way. But don't blame me when you finally get home and I'm already on the sofa in prime telly-watching position. Bye."

The truth was, the chances of finding a wormhole in Gilmour Park – or anywhere, in fact – were practically zero. But, thought Harry, you never knew. Incredible coincidences and strange things did happen.

Harry was about to discover how true that was.

By a not so incredible non-coincidence, there wasn't a wormhole under the see-saw. Harry was a little disappointed, but soon forgot about it when, coming out of the park on to a quiet side road, he saw a young man sitting in a car pointing a camera at Geddy's Café on the main road.

If that roused Harry's curiosity (which it did), what happened next sent it into orbit. The man in the car seemed to be taking pictures of another man, who was drinking a mug of tea at a window table in the café. A man who just happened to be Gus Moore, Harry and Abby's father.

Harry went and stood directly in front of the man's camera, blocking his view so that all he could probably see now was blue, the colour of Harry's school jumper.

The man, who had short brown hair with a parting to one side and was wearing dark glasses, initially seemed to think that there was something wrong with his camera. He looked at it and then shook it a couple of times.

Harry decided that more direct action was called for, so he tapped on the car's window. The man jumped and rolled it down.

"Erm, what are you doing?" said Harry.

"Nothing," said the man. "Nothing at all. Absolutely nothing."

"You're not doing *nothing*," retorted Harry. "You're in a car, pointing a camera at my dad. Which is definitely something."

And that takes us back to. . .

"Please don't tell anyone you've seen me. Please, please, please, pleaaaaaaaasssssssseeeee!"

Yeah. Awkward.

"OK, OK, I won't," said a stunned and bemused

Harry. "But I've worked it out anyway. You're from a celebrity magazine, aren't you? You're doing a 'Where Are They Now?' thing on my father."

Harry's guess was based on two things: the fact that his father used to be famous, and the fact that his father was now not famous at all.

Gus Moore had once been Britain's funniest man. He'd started out as a stand-up comedian before starring in the TV comedy *A Right Pickle*, about a pickle-maker who was always getting into a pickle. It ran for five series and was so successful that the final episode was watched by everyone in the country apart from two old ladies in Sheerness who'd locked themselves out after they'd popped to the shops to buy some pickles.

Hollywood came calling after that and Gus starred in a number of movies, notably *Boing!*, the story of a rubber band manufacturer stretched to his limit, and *Boing 2!*, about a giraffe with superpowers.

Then, at the peak of Gus Moore's career, disaster struck. As so often happens in a marriage when one half of the couple is hugely successful and the other stays home and brings up the children, Gus's wife, Samantha, robbed a bank.

No one knew quite what happened. Samantha said she'd only gone in to order a new cash card, but then somehow found herself writing, *I have a weapon in my bag. Give me all your money. Please*, on a piece of paper and giving it to the teller. Even though the "weapon" was a cucumber, she walked out with £3,415.79 and had just purchased a deluxe gold-leaf cat flap when she was arrested.

The first thing Gus said when he found out was, "But we don't have a cat."

When it came to trial Samantha found herself up against Judge Lillian "Lock 'Em Up" Baxter, a tough, no-nonsense judge who also happened to hate cucumber, which was almost certainly part of the reason she sentenced Samantha to five years in prison.

To begin with, Gus hired a nanny to look after Harry and Abby and used the robbery in his comedy routines – "Yes, it was a real surprise, totally unexpected. She told me she was going to rob the *post office*."

Six months later, though, four nannies had left – two

because Gus forgot to pay them, one because he'd accidentally locked her in the toilet overnight and one because he hadn't given her a set of keys (she lasted fifteen seconds and didn't even enter the house).

Gus was trying to hire a fifth nanny when he opened a newspaper to see a story about what a terrible person he was. "Worst Dad of the Year," it said. The story had been sold to the paper by the nanny who'd lasted fifteen seconds, which didn't seem fair, but social media went nuts – #worstdadever was trending. Gus felt awful, and so he decided to give up comedy and stay home to look after the twins (though the reality was very much the other way round).

That was four years ago; probably, Harry thought, the right amount of time for celebrity magazines to run a "Where Are They Now?" story on Gus.

As guesses go, it was pretty good. But, it turned out, not good enough.

"Actually you're wrong," said the man, triumphantly taking off his dark glasses. "I'm with the secret service and I'm on a top-secret assignment! It's only my third day, in fact."

Suddenly the man's look of triumph turned to panic. "Oh no," he squealed. "All I've done since I joined the service eighteen months ago is sit at a desk and fill in forms. If they find out that I've been spotted – and by you! The child of my target! – I'll be back there in no time. That's why you really can't say a word to anyone."

"Sorry, did you say the secret service?" asked a confused Harry.

The man clapped a hand over his mouth. "Please don't tell anyone that either," he said through his fingers.

Harry's mind was now going ballistic. He seemed to have stumbled across the world's worst spy, who for some reason was spying (very badly) on his dad. This was *ten times* better than discovering a wormhole.

He was just about to assure the man that he wouldn't say anything to anyone (apart from Abby, of course) when there was a loud crash, a scream, some shouting and a lot of apologizing.

It was coming from Geddy's Café and, glancing over, Harry could see his father frantically apologizing to a woman at another table. If Harry had to make another guess, he'd have said that the crash was caused by his father standing up and catching his knees under the table, which knocked over his half-full cup, pouring its contents into the woman's handbag. That would account for the scream, followed by the shouting, and the apologizing.

This time Harry's guess was pretty good. In fact, in an exam it would have been given 97 per cent (the cup was only a third full).

Shaking his head, Harry turned back to the spy. "Look," he said. "I'll keep your mission secret, but you have to tell me what it has to do with my dad."

"Fine," said the spy. "But not now. Not here. Too many ears, if you get my meaning. You and your sister meet me this time tomorrow by the playground in the park. I'll explain everything then."

"OK," said Harry.

"Great. I'll say, 'What's the weather like?' and you reply, 'It is not raining in Tokyo.' Got it?"

"Err. Why?" said Harry.

"Because that's what we do in the secret service," said the man a little irritably. "Right, don't forget, same time tomorrow. Synchronize watches."

"I don't wear a watch," said Harry.

"Well, synchronize someone else's watch," the man said, starting the car and driving off, leaving Harry more intrigued and excited than if he'd discovered ten wormholes, three black holes and a large chunk of that Swiss cheese full of holes.

CHAPTER 2

The Things You Hear on a Park Bench

"Look, I know it sounds odd. OK, very odd. But it's true! Honestly. If I'm lying, I'll give you my pocket money for the next fifty years."

Abby doubted that Harry would still be getting pocket money when he was sixty-three, but there was something about how persuasive he was being that made her think there might just be some truth in his mad story. That, and the twin thing of knowing-without-knowing. Despite being very different, they still had that connection that exists between two people who have played sardines inside their mother for nine months.

That was why, despite her better instincts, Abby found herself sitting with Harry on the bench in Gilmour Park on a cloudy afternoon, the sort of day where the sun plays hide-and-seek with the clouds, very occasionally popping out from behind them, and then disappearing again for ages.

"Are you sure he wanted to meet here and not actually in Tokyo?" said Abby.

"Why would he want to meet in Tokyo?" said Harry.

"Why does he want to meet us at all?!" snapped Abby. "And he's late."

"I told you," said Harry. "He's not a very good spy."

"I blooming well am!" said a voice behind the twins. "And I'm only late because my watch fell in a puddle and is running a little slow."

"It is not raining in Tokyo," said Harry, turning round. The spy was wearing a dark suit and carrying a briefcase. He'd clearly also had trouble with his tie – the knot was far too big and one end was almost touching his left knee.

"What?" said the spy.

"That's what you told me to say," replied Harry.

"Yes, but I was meant to say 'What's the weather like' first."

"Oh yes," said Harry. "Go on then."

"Look," interrupted Abby. "Could you just explain what's going on and why you were spying on our dad yesterday?"

"OK, OK," said the spy, plonking himself down next to Harry and Abby on the bench. "Let me introduce myself first, though. I'm Agent 4905-3. Or you can call me Trevor."

"We're Harry and Abby," said Harry.

"I know," said Trevor, smiling mysteriously. "But keep your voices down, there could be double agents and moles close by."

"Oh, there won't be any moles," said Harry. "The park keeper got rid of them last year."

"What?" said Trevor.

"Ignore him," said Abby. "He's trying to be funny. It runs in the family. Go on."

Agent 4905-3 did indeed go on, and what he said was unquestionably the most exciting thing that had happened to them since . . . since *ever*.

Agent 4905-3 cleared his throat and began.

"As I'm sure you know, the new series of *BBNS*, *Britain's Biggest New Star*, is starting soon. It was once the biggest TV show in the country, but the last two series haven't done so well in the ratings, so they've been trying to get people excited about this new one. Lots of ads on TV, that sort of thing. Then, about six weeks ago, a video came out online which *really* got everyone talking."

Harry and Abby were about to say they'd seen it, but the agent just carried on and told them about it anyway.

"It was a video of a dog. A chocolate-brown Labrador. You know, one of those ones with big floppy ears, gentle eyes and a wet-looking nose. It was lying on a cushion when suddenly it sat up and, looking straight in to the camera, it started talking, would you believe?

"'The new series of *Britain's Biggest New Star* must not go ahead,' said the Labrador. 'It must be cancelled or powers from beyond the grave will unleash a terrible curse!'"

"It then lay down again and went back to sleep.

"Now, it may interest you to know that dogs can't actually talk and if it had been just ANY dog, no one would have cared. But this dog, who is called Greta, just happened to belong to one of the show's judges, famous comedian Clive Derek, and she also sounded just like him.

"So lots of people saw it and of course, everyone thought it must be a publicity stunt, but Clive denied all knowledge of the video. He said that it was nothing to do with him, but he always knew Greta was very intelligent.

"The other three judges – actress Eve Cotton, pop star Diamond and talent agent Wally Deighton, who created the show – then got in on the act by very publicly arguing that their pets were just as intelligent, even though Eve only has a goldfish and Wally doesn't actually have a pet.

"Now, if it *had* been a publicity stunt organized by the show, they would have been patting themselves on the back, because interest in the new series was now sky high. But it wasn't. The show's producers had nothing to do with the video and had no idea who had made it or why.

"Then some other weird things started happening. The satnav in the senior producer's car started speaking in a spooky voice and directing her to cemeteries. The director's phone rang in the middle of the night and when she answered it, she heard Sir David Attenborough talking about how, if the show went ahead, directors would be extinct by the end of the year. And the show's host, Mac Tatum, put a bath on to run, and when he returned to it the water was green and full of worms.

"The public weren't told about these other weird happenings, and everyone working on the show was sworn to secrecy. The producers were a bit worried, but thought it was probably some disgruntled ex-contestant who had had their fun and would now stop, but then something else happened. Diamond went to bed one night and was woken up at three in the morning by someone singing her hit song, 'Ooh Aah La La La'. Only in this version, the lyrics had been changed and the person was singing, 'Ooh aah, beware the final, ooh aah the curse will strike.'

"Now the producers were *really* worried because a special *royal* guest is due to attend the final.

"That was when they decided to call the secret service and ask them to investigate. And, as luck would have it, I answered that call. I'm a big fan of the show. I even considered auditioning myself, once – but I wasn't sure my comedy songs were quite up to scratch.

"Anyway, my bosses were more than happy to let me take the case. Most of them don't even know what *BBNS* is, and so putting an expert like myself in charge made perfect sense."

"Wow," said Harry and Abby at exactly the same time.

They were quiet for a moment, thinking about everything Trevor had said.

"Curses aren't real," said Abby at last. "This is just someone trying to sabotage the show."

"But why would someone want to?" asked Harry.

"Who knows how the criminal mind works," said

Trevor. "But I'm going to find out. Which is why I was watching your father."

"O . . . kay," said Abby. She was feeling a strange mix of emotions. She was a naturally cautious person, but part of her had always liked the idea of being a spy, and that part was currently getting quite excited. "Go on."

"*My* idea," went on Trevor excitedly, "is to get someone undercover on the show."

"How?" said Harry

"Well," said Trevor, lowering his voice a little. "They'll be a contestant but they'll really be working undercover for us so they can find out who is behind everything that's been happening. And stop them, of course."

"And you think that person should be our father?" said Harry.

"Totally," said Trevor, excitedly whipping off his dark glasses. "He's a genius. A brilliant comedian, an amazing entertainer, just a huge, huge talent. I lov— Erm, I like him very much. He's perfect for the job."

"Right," said Abby slowly. "And you think being a brilliant comedian and entertainer are the qualities an undercover agent needs? Rather than, say, intelligence, awareness and the ability to stay calm under pressure?"

"None of which our father possesses," added Harry.

"Look," said Trevor. "Whoever we choose has to be believable, and they need to be talented enough to stay on the show. I mean, someone in the office suggested we use Molly Glover, you know, that singer from that show a little while back. Sure, she had a couple of minor hits and somehow got to the final of *Celebrity Mastermind*. But I have more talent in my nose hairs! It was ridiculous. But then after I'd shown everyone in the office every episode of your father's comedy show and all his live DVDs, along with some unreleased footage I got at an auction for only three thousand pounds – they knew I was right."

Abby looked at Harry, and their shared twin thought was: Trevor was not just a fan of their father's. He was an uber-fan verging on bonkers, who was probably only choosing their father for this assignment because he might get to meet him, rather than because their father was the right person for the job.

"Anyway, my plan to let Harry catch me yesterday worked," said Trevor.

"Oh," said Abby. "So you knew Harry would be coming out of the back entrance of the park because he'd been searching for wormholes?"

"Yes, yes," said Trevor irritably. "Anyway, I was having some concerns about using your father. Like a lot of brilliant geniuses, he can be a little, erm, erratic."

"You mean that he's very clumsy and so wrapped up in himself that he doesn't take any interest in or notice anything else," said Abby.

"Something like that, yes," said Trevor. "Anyway, because of that my idea is . . . and always was . . . for you two to be there backstage at the show to, erm, keep an eye on things."

"By which you mean our father," said Abby. "You want us to make sure he doesn't tell everyone what he's doing. And at the same time we can make sure he doesn't fall down some stairs while he's trying to stay undercover."

"It would just be a precaution," said Trevor. "We have someone on the inside, one of the show's producers. Josie Jubb. Her uncle used to be in the service, so she's definitely OK. She's the only one who knows the specific details of my plan. If too many people know what Gus is really doing, they might blow his cover. She'll make contact with him on the show."

"And make sure he doesn't get knocked out of the competition too early," said Abby.

"Don't be ridiculous," said Trevor, looking shocked. "That would never happen. Anyway, my point is, you'd just be an extra pair of eyes. It wouldn't be a proper assignment for you two because it's against secret service policy to use children as agents. Rule fourteen, paragraph three, sub-section eight of the regulations, I think. Or it might be section nine. And paragraph four..."

"Excuse me, Trevor," said Harry, interrupting smoothly. "I think your plan is amazing, brilliant in fact. Wouldn't you agree, Abby?"

"Yes, absolutely," said Abby, eyeing Harry suspiciously. She knew he was up to something.

"But one thing worries me," Harry went on. "This is obviously a risky assignment. There's someone out there who is desperate to destroy the show. If something were to happen to Gus, the world would lose a genius. That would be terrible."

"Yes, it would," said Trevor, looking appalled.

"Plus," went on Harry, "if he's wandering around and poking his nose into places he's not meant to be instead of focusing on his performance, I'd give it about a day before everyone guesses what he's up to."

Trevor nodded and fiddled with his large tie knot in quite a worried way. "Hmm, yes," he said. "That could be a problem."

"But fear not," said Harry. "I have an idea. Why don't you make me and Abby the actual undercover agents?"

"What?" said Trevor, far too loudly for a spy.

"We're really very sensible," said Harry. "And at thirteen we're practically grown-ups. The contestants always get to bring family members along – no one would suspect a thing. Plus you'd get two for the price of one."

"That's true," said Trevor. "But it's not allowed. As I said, rule fourteen, paragraph three, or maybe four, sub-section eight or maybe nine clearly states. . ."

"Oh, I'm sure you can bend the rules a bit," said Abby, who for once in her life thought that Harry had come up with a brilliant idea. "After all, what is the secret service best at?"

"Erm, well, the biscuits in the canteen are very good," said Trevor.

"I'm sure they are," said Abby patiently. "But I'm talking about *secrets*. Keeping secrets. And this can be ours. No one need ever know."

"I, er, I still, I, well, erm," spluttered Trevor.

"And then of course," said Harry, "this competition might turn Gus into a star again. There will be more tours, more DVDs, more opportunities for photos, autographs, you name it. You might even get a *private* interview."

Trevor's eyes lit up.

"Right," he said, trying to sound professional even though he was as excited as ten bulls in a china shop. "I have thought about what you've said and decided that it could work. As you say, it would have to be a secret, our secret. No one, not even your father, could know anything about it."

Harry and Abby nodded vigorously.

"And you will report directly to me, and only me. Agreed?"

"Agreed," said Abby and Harry together.

"Good," said Trevor. "So the first thing you need to do is convince Gus to sign up for the show."

"No problem," said Harry with a juggernaut-sized amount of overconfidence. "He'll be like putty in our hands. Two weeks and we'll have him *begging* to take part in the show."

"Ah," said Trevor. "Just one thing. We don't have two weeks. The deadline for entering is five p.m. tomorrow."

CHAPTER 3
The Plan

"Oh, ha ha, that is brilliant, Dad!" said Abby, wiping a tear from her eye. "Harry, come and hear Dad's hilarious joke!"

Harry, who had been waiting outside the room, bounded in, a look of carefully manufactured expectancy on his face.

"Well," said Gus. "George from next door popped round and when he left he said, 'I'm off.' To which I replied, 'You've been off for years.'"

"Oh, ha ha ha, that's great, Dad," said Harry, doubling over and holding his sides. "He meant off like, he's going, but you changed it to mean off like mouldy food. Brilliant! You should tweet it, it'll go viral."

"Erm, yes, maybe I will," said Gus, looking puzzled. He had a sense that something wasn't quite right, but he couldn't put his finger on exactly what.

That joke was one of Gus's classic Dad jokes. He'd probably made it ten thousand times before, and aside from the first time they'd heard it aged seven, Harry and Abby had never reacted with anything more than a slight chuckle.

But then, Gus didn't know about The Plan. Specifically, The Plan to Get Dad to Sign Up for *Britain's Biggest New Star*.

There were three parts.

Part One: convince Dad that he was still as funny as he'd ever been, funnier in fact.

This should have been easy. All Harry and Abby had to do was laugh at any attempt at humour Gus made. Actually, it was excruciatingly difficult.

As everyone knows, your own dad is just not funny, even if he's a comedian. Whenever a dad tries to be funny, all his kids feel is irritated, embarrassed and a little sick. So Harry and Abby were finding Part One of The Plan very difficult. In fact, when they laughed, an outside observer might think they were actually in pain. Their seventy-eight-year-old neighbour, George, certainly did. He even thought about coming back over to check everything was OK – but he decided on a cup of tea instead.

On the plus side, though, Gus had an ego the size of Jupiter. It was so big that he still thought he was the funniest man on television (even though he hadn't been *on* television for four years). This meant that any doubts he may have had about his children laughing at his jokes were quickly swept aside by his assumption that he was a comedy god.

Part Two: show Gus how independent Harry and Abby were, so that he wouldn't think, *I can't return to comedy, my children can't cope without me.* It was ridiculous really. Harry and Abby had pretty much been looking after *him* for the past four years, something that, because of Gus's vast ego, he might not have realized.

So far for Part Two, Abby and Harry had made Gus breakfast and lunch, washed up breakfast and lunch, ironed his shirts, hung out the washing, hoovered the house, dusted, changed the beds, watered the plants and regrouted some tiles in the bathroom, even though they didn't need regrouting.

What with doing all that, making sure Gus knew they had done all that, and laughing at all of Gus's jokes, it had been an exhausting day for the twins. Harry, in particular, was desperate to move on to Part Three.

"I can't do it any more," whined Harry when Gus had wandered off. "Laughing at Dad's jokes is killing me."

"Come on, Agent Harry," said Abby in a stern voice. "Stiff upper lip. Remember, you're doing this for Queen and country."

"My upper lip is so stiff from fake laughing I can barely move it. Can't we move on to Part Three?"

Abby sighed. "OK, but if it doesn't work, we'll have to activate the emergency plan: crying real tears of laughter. I've got some onions on standby."

They found Dad making tea in the kitchen.

"Hey, Dad, you know what?" said Abby.

"Yes, I know What very well," said Gus. "We went to school together."

"Oh, ha ha ha," cackled Abby as Harry made a noise like a strangled duck.

Abby gave it another few seconds and then continued. "The new series of *BBNS* is starting soon, isn't it?"

"Is it?" said Gus, dropping his teabag in the bin.

"It is. We were watching some clips from the last series yesterday. The comedians on it were OK, but we think you're a million times better."

"Ah, well," said Gus. "Comedy's not like it was back

in the old days."

"But it could be, Dad," said Harry.

"Yes, it could be," said Gus. "If you had a time machine, Harry."

The twins laughed heartily again. Abby sounded like a constipated donkey this time. Then Harry wiped a non-existent tear from his eye and continued.

"I haven't got a time machine, Dad," he said. "But you wouldn't need one if you entered *BBNS* yourself."

"Oh, Harry, what an amazing idea," said Abby. "It would be the perfect opportunity for a comeback."

"And," said Harry before Gus could get a word in, "when you win, because you will, obvs, it'll put you right back on the comedy map, not to mention you'd get a big cash prize."

Gus frowned and thought for a minute.

"Maybe you're right," he said. "But why bother with *BBNS*? It's been losing ratings for years. My shows were huge. I was nominated for a Golden Globe. An arena tour would be a better way to announce my comeback. I could do a two-hour show of new stuff, which my fans would love!"

The twins stared at him.

"That's – that's a brilliant idea, Dad. Isn't it, Harry?" said Abby at last.

Harry nodded in agreement even though he didn't know why he was agreeing with it.

"*But*," said Abby, "you haven't done a tour in a while, have you, Dad? People might need a tiny reminder of who you are – I mean, how great you are..."

"Hmm," Gus muttered thoughtfully.

"Going on *BBNS* would do the trick," said Abby firmly. "After hearing a few minutes of new material, your fans will be desperate for more. The tour will sell out in seconds. It's perfect."

There was silence. Abby and Harry looked at their father, trying to work out what was going on in his head. It could have been anything from "I'm going to do it" to "I wonder what's for supper?" to "Why did the chicken cross the road?"

Incredibly, it was none of those things.

When Gus spoke again, he said, "My fans *do* deserve to see me again. But don't you think we should talk to Mum about this?"

Harry and Abby were stunned. It wasn't like Gus to think about someone else. To be fair, in all the excitement, they hadn't thought about their mother either.

A moment later Harry and Abby were stunned again, along with Gus, when a voice said:

"Talk to me about what?"

The three of them swung round to see their mother, Samantha, standing in the kitchen doorway wearing an orange prison jumpsuit.

"Oh, Mum!" shouted Harry. "Not again. How many times have you escaped now?"

Samantha shrugged. She didn't know exactly how many times she'd escaped from prison, but she knew it was a lot.

Escaping from prison is something that you don't find out you're good at until you actually end up in prison. Samantha Moore, as it turned out, was VERY good at it.

Samantha was in a Category C prison, which wasn't high security, but equally wasn't made of paper. The first time she escaped was by accident. In her second week there she'd fallen asleep in a pile of laundry and woken up in a dry cleaner's fourteen miles away. After that, there was no stopping her and she started devising ever more creative ways to break out.

This time she'd dug a hole in the floor of her cell, with a huge pile of dirt next to it. All the guards had jumped down the tunnel, but Samantha was actually hiding in the dirt. When that was tipped into a bin and then into a dustcart, she was soon on the outside.

Samantha thought that escaping was great fun, but unfortunately the authorities didn't, and each time she was caught – or went back herself, which she did quite a lot – her sentence was increased.

"Nice work regrouting the bathroom tiles, by the way, Gus," said Samantha, ignoring Harry's question.

"Er, thank you," mumbled Gus, wondering when he had done that.

"So," said Samantha. "What do you want to talk to me about?"

Harry, Abby and Gus told Samantha all about *BBNS*. Then they waited, uncertainly, for a response from her. She was often quite unpredictable, as the unfortunate bank teller had discovered, so it was anyone's guess how she would react.

"I love the idea," she exclaimed finally.

"You do?" said Gus.

"Of course," said Samantha. "Every time you come to see me you moan about how much you miss being onstage. Habby" – her nickname for the twins – "should probably start doing more around the house too – you're always saying how exhausted you are."

"Well, that is wonderful, darling," said a mightily relieved Gus. "Isn't it, children?"

It took a moment for Habby to respond, as they were both seething. Gus did *no* housework. In fact, he made more for them. But they didn't say anything. They didn't want to scupper the plan.

"Just one thing, though," said Samantha, with a wicked twinkle in her eye. "What's in it for me?"

"Sorry, darling," said Gus. "What do you mean?"

"Well, you'll be getting all famous again and getting invited to all sorts of fancy-pants parties. What do *I* get out of it?"

"Ah, well, yes, I, er, I mean, we have given that some

thought, haven't we, Abby?" spluttered Gus.

"Actually, I do have an idea about that, Mum," said Abby thoughtfully.

"Oh, I was only kidding, I just wanted to see the look on your father's face," said Samantha. "Right, must go, I promised Brenda the Fence I'd be back in our cell by five for a game of hide-and-seek. See you later."

Mum departed much as she'd arrived, quietly and suddenly. A relieved and exhausted Harry was just about to flop down on a chair when he caught sight of the clock.

"It's twenty to five! The deadline to enter is five! Come on, Dad. You've got twenty minutes."

Nineteen minutes and seventeen seconds later, Gus pressed *send* on the application form. Habby breathed a sigh of relief. The Plan had gone to plan. Gus had signed up to an assignment with the secret service – and he didn't even know it.

As Gus headed upstairs to work on material for the first round of auditions, Abby and Harry looked at each other. Now it was time for the really hard work to begin. They were going undercover.

CHAPTER 4
Looking (Not Quite So) Rosy

"Gus, why have you decided to enter *BBNS* after all this time?"

"Gus, can I get a picture?"

"Gus, will you be doing any jokes about pickles?"

"Gus, why are your shoelaces undone?"

These questions and more were screeched at Gus as he made his way past the hordes of photographers and journalists and into the *BBNS* studio building for the first live show.

It had been pretty easy, Gus thought, to land a spot on *BBNS*. He'd had to make a one-minute audition tape, which the judges had loved, and, after a short discussion, they'd put him into the first live show, along with twenty-nine others. If he got through this stage, he'd be in the semi-final, just one step away from the final itself.

Harry and Abby were walking a few paces behind him. They were especially keen not to draw attention to themselves, as Trevor had fully kitted them out with hidden recording devices and concealed cameras with which to gather evidence.

With other contestants and their families also filing in, it was so noisy that Gus didn't hear the question about his shoelaces and instead tripped and went flying into the woman in front of him. She was carrying ten chickens in a basket (her act involved chickens playing a xylophone) and as Harry and Abby watched in horror, the basket flew open and the chickens made a bid for freedom. The twins had no option but to help retrieve them, which is how they ended up in the paper the next day under the headline CLUCKY ESCAPE.

It was also noisy because of the other people there.

As the twins returned the last chicken, they saw them, a large group holding signs and shouting.

"I recognize her," whispered Abby, gesturing towards a young woman with long, bright red hair and green eyes at the front of the group. "That's Debbie Acorn."

"Debbie who?" said Harry.

"Debbie Acorn. She's the host of *Wooooooooooooo*, that online paranormal ghost show. It's pretty big."

"Do not walk through those doors!" cried Debbie, pointing a trembling finger towards the studio. "The spirits have spoken through Greta. Heed their warning or you will all pay a terrible price!"

She was brandishing a sign that read, BBNS = BRITAIN BE NERVOUS AND SCARED, while the others around her showed their support by shouting, "Yeah" and "Go, Debbie!" and "Beware the curse!"

"What a weirdo," said Harry.

"Maybe," said Abby, looking at Debbie thoughtfully. "Let's just get inside without anything else happening."

They hurried into the studio building, gently nudging Gus forward as they did so.

In the foyer a member of the show's production team gave them a pass each and then directed them to a large room marked CONTESTANTS' WAITING AREA.

The rest of the building consisted of various offices and technical rooms, a canteen and of course, a large stage area. Everything looked very clean and bright, which, as the show staff member explained, was because it was a brand-new studio building that they were using for the first time.

The waiting area was a teeming hive of activity. There were people everywhere. People in weird costumes, people dancing, singing, talking to themselves, stretching, balancing and juggling. There were animals – mainly dogs, but also chickens, obvs, a couple of monkeys and a small horse. There were camera operators filming and an army of staff and producers shouting, being shouted at, asking questions, being asked questions and generally trying to act as if they knew what was going on.

Eventually Harry, Abby and Gus battled through the throng and found some chairs.

"What's she up to?" said Harry, once Gus had settled down to work on his routine. "The girl with the sign. Could she have made the video and done all those other things to try and stop the show?"

"Seems unlikely. I'd say she's just sensed an

opportunity to get publicity for *her* show," said Abby. "Her ratings have gone through the roof since all this *BBNS* stuff has started." She glanced around. "Do you think our cover has been blown?"

"I think one of the chickens might have seen my hidden microphone," said Harry. "But I don't reckon she'll talk."

"Shut up, Harry," said Abby, who was in no mood for jokes. "Right, time for a quick Trevor check."

Discreetly, Abby felt for the microphone attached to her arm and pressed a button on it.

"Abby to Agent 4905-3," she whispered. There was silence. "Abby to Trevor, come in, Trevor."

Still nothing. Abby was about to try again when a loud static cackle burst out of the tiny earpieces they were wearing, making her and Harry jump violently. Thankfully, the only people who noticed thought they were a breakdancing act.

"What do you mean, come in?" barked Trevor. "I can't come in, I'm in a van half a mile away."

"I was just testing the equipment, Trevor – I mean, Agent 4905-3. To check you can hear us," said Abby.

"Well, go on then," said Trevor.

"Erm, right," said Abby. "This is Abby. Can you hear me?"

"Yes," said Trevor.

"This is Harry, can you hear me?"

"Yes," said Trevor. "And this is Agent 4905-3. Can *you* hear *me*?"

Harry and Abby shook their heads. "Yes," they said together.

"Good," said Trevor. "Now, we are standing by . . . well, I'm actually *sitting* at the moment, but . . . oh yes, please. Two sugars, thanks. Where was I? Oh, and I'll have a chocolate biscuit too if there's one going."

Harry and Abby looked at each other and, without speaking, decided it was best to let Trevor get on with Operation Tea and Choccy Biccie for the time being.

"Right," said Abby. "All Dad has to do now is wait till he's called. So we should split up and chat to as many people as we can and report back on anything suspicious."

"OK," said Harry. "Meet back here in half an hour."

The twins looked up and, at the same time, both took a deep breath. The mass of people in the waiting area had got even bigger, and whilst heading off into them wasn't quite like going into a war zone, it didn't seem far off it.

"Good luck," said Harry.

"Good . . . oh no," said Abby. "Look."

Harry looked up and saw four producers parting the sea of contestants so that the show's host, Mac Tatum, and the judge Clive Derek could walk through them.

Mac was thirty-three and looked confident and smart in a sharp blue suit that matched his piercing eyes. He had the sort of face that could be described as chiselled – a strong jawline, high, defined cheekbones and a large, prominent forehead with short, light brown hair on top. It took a lot of highly skilled make-up artists for him to look like that, and the few people who got to see him pre-chisel knew that he actually looked quite different, something they kept to themselves.

Clive, who was about the same age as Gus, also looked quite smart in just a casual shirt and trousers, but he was a broader, bigger man. His face was quite round, with big ears that jutted out from beneath his messy, free-flowing hair.

They were making a beeline for Gus, who was currently picking chicken feathers out of his beard.

"Maybe we should stick around," said Abby. "See what they want."

"Yeah," said Harry. "And it was Clive's dog in the video, so he's definitely worth keeping an eye on."

"Hey, hey, hey," shouted Mac. "If it isn't the funniest man on the planet, Gus Moore!"

To the children's amazement, Gus instantly transformed from a guy messing about with his beard into a full-on celebrity. It was almost magical.

"Mac, great to see you, buddy," he said, beaming. "Fancy seeing you here, of all places."

"Didn't I tell you this guy was funny, Clive?" said Mac, slapping Gus on the back and laughing.

"Actually, you said he was a desperate washed-up has-been," said Clive.

Harry and Abby winced at that, but Gus guffawed as if it was hilarious. He knew Mac and Clive well from when they'd been on shows together in the past and seemed to have forgotten that things were a little different now.

"Good one, Clive," said Gus. "Listen, no one's shown me to my dressing room yet. Where is it?"

Mac and Clive doubled up again, but the twins knew it hadn't been a joke.

"Seriously, though," said Mac, speaking quietly now. "*My* dressing room is the best in the building, and it's miles away from the rabble. I told them I needed absolute peace and quiet before a show. There isn't even a phone in there."

"Great," said Gus. "And mine is . . . ?"

"So any time you need some R and R," continued

Mac, ignoring his question, "come by and we can have a good chat about the old days. And I don't make that offer to just anyone. If Clive comes within a hundred metres of my room, security are on him in a flash."

Mac and Clive creased up again at that, though Gus wasn't laughing this time. The twins guessed he'd realized he wasn't getting a dressing room.

"Abs," whispered Harry. "Maybe one of us should try to talk to Clive. About the dog."

"Good idea," whispered Abby. "Dad can introduce us and. . ."

"Hey, I remember these two rascals! Henry! Abby! How are you?"

Startled, the twins looked up to find Mac's face right in front of them. His perfect teeth were so white they almost had to cover their eyes.

"It's Harry, actually," said Harry, but he might as well have said it to the chickens.

"Great, great," said Mac. "Now then, it's good of you to come and support your dad, but he's a pro, and from what I've heard he can still feed himself, so I'm sure he'll be fine, which means you guys could do me a little favour."

The way Mac said it, it didn't seem as though Harry and Abby had much choice.

"My niece is staying with me for a while – my sister and her husband have just set off to pogo stick round the world for charity. She's a lovely girl, but very ... quiet. A bit shy. She's worried about all this cursing business. I've told her it's nonsense, but she could use some company to take her mind off it. Now where is she? Rosy? Rosy? Ah, there you are."

The twins looked around. At first they couldn't see anyone, but then, peering out from behind one of the producers, they saw a girl.

"Come on, sweetheart," said Mac. "Don't be shy, come and meet Henry and Abby."

Gently but firmly, the producer eased Rosy forward.

She was probably about ten or eleven, with brown hair in pigtails. She was wearing a pink dress and squeezing a small teddy bear so tightly a giant with a crowbar would have had trouble prising it off her.

"Now, Rosy," said Mac. "This is Henry and Abby. Their father is my *great* friend Gus."

"It's Harry," muttered Harry again, but Mac just

carried on.

"I have loads of boring work to do, so they've kindly said you can 'hang' with them, isn't that nice? You'll have lots of fun *and* they've promised to keep you safe from the curse!"

Harry and Abby didn't remember saying either of those things.

"Well, got to dash now, sooooo busy. See you all in a bit," said Mac, departing hurriedly with Clive.

Harry and Abby stared at the girl in front of them as she nestled her freckled face into her teddy. They knew precisely what the other was thinking.

How on earth did that just happen? And why was this shy and slightly odd girl their problem now?

They also knew that their undercover task had suddenly become considerably more difficult.

CHAPTER 5

A Spanner in the Works

"So, erm, good to meet you, Rosy," said Abby.

"Yes, good to meet you," echoed Harry.

Rosy gave no indication that she'd heard the twins. Her eyes were fixed firmly downwards, as if she'd much rather be having a conversation with the floor.

"Who's this?" said Abby, pointing to the teddy bear.

Rosy's lips moved, but she didn't look up.

"Sorry, I didn't hear you," said Abby.

This time Rosy managed to lift her chin away from her chest and whisper something in a voice a bat with a hearing aid would struggle to hear.

"Freddy?" said Abby. "That's a nice name."

Now Rosy did look up properly.

"No," she said, quite clearly and a bit crossly. "Not Freddy. Teddy."

"Of course it's Teddy," said Harry. "My sister has got such cloth ears. I once asked her for a cup of tea, and she thought I said a cup of wee."

Rosy tilted her head to one side and looked at Harry. A confused frown spread across her forehead. Then she burst out laughing.

Harry and Abby started laughing as well, whilst at the same time, breathing a sigh of relief. She had a sense of humour, even if she was carrying a teddy bear.

Having broken the ice, Harry was about to ask Rosy if she'd ever been to the show before when the whole studio resounded to a bellowing shriek of, "LOOK OUT!!"

The next moment something crashed down in front of them, missing Rosy by the width of a gnat's little toenail.

In the stunned silence that followed, Abby saw that it was a large and very heavy spanner.

Everyone began talking at once. Even the chickens were squawking excitedly, which made for quite a stew of noise.

A lot of people were looking up and pointing to where they thought the spanner had come from.

"Abby," said Harry, scanning the ceiling himself. "What just happened?"

"I don't exactly know," said Abby. "Rosy, are you all right?"

Rosy had turned very pale and looked as if she might be sick. "I ... think so," she whispered.

"Sorry, sorry. I'm so sorry. Are you OK?" came a voice.

They looked round to see a man in a T-shirt and shorts with a tool belt around his waist. He had short, dark hair and his arms were covered in tattoos.

"I'm so sorry," he said again, wiping sweat from his forehead. "I'm Tom, the handyman here. I was fixing a light. I don't know how that could have happened." He stared at the spanner, shaking his head.

A producer came running over. He was a burly man with short hair and a big beard.

"Hi, I'm Mikey. Is everyone all right?" he said. "Rosy?"

The colour still hadn't quite returned to Rosy's face, but she nodded and said she was OK.

"It's so weird," Tom said. "I always, always check that my tools are securely attached. And I definitely checked this time too. It's never happened before. . . I can't understand it."

"I can," said a singer, a look of horror in her eyes. "It was a ghost. The curse has struck."

"Don't be ridiculous," said a one-man band, clanking over. "That's all nonsense, just publicity for the show. This was an accident."

"Was it?" said a juggler. "He said it's never happened before. Bit of a coincidence that it should happen now, isn't it?"

Suddenly everyone was discussing whether the Mysterious Incident of the Falling Spanner was just an accident, or the work of ghosts, ghouls, phantoms or the angry spirit of a ballerina who had once performed at these studios and stubbed her toe quite badly.

"OK, OK," shouted Mikey above the clamour. "Can everyone just calm down?"

The chatter slowly subsided.

"Thank you," he said. "I'm sure there's a perfectly straightforward explanation for what happened, but in the meantime, you all have a show to prepare for, so can I suggest you concentrate on that?"

That did the trick and the room returned to its previous slightly less excitable state.

"You'd better come to first aid with me, Rosy," said Mikey. "Just to be on the safe side."

"I don't need first aid," said Rosy. "It didn't hit me."

"I really think it would be best if we had you thoroughly checked over," said Mikey. "It won't take long, you'll be back with your friends soon."

Rosy huffed a little.

"See you later," she said to the twins as she followed Mikey out.

The minute Rosy left, Harry and Abby turned to

each other.

"What do you think?" said Harry. "Sabotage? Ghost? Curse?"

"I don't know," said Abby. "Well, I *do* know. It wasn't a ghost or anything like that. But was it just an accident?"

"Hmm," hmm-ed Harry. "I managed to get a photo of Tom. Trevor can run it through their computers and see if he has any previous."

"Previous what?" said Abby. "Previous instances when he nearly dropped a heavy spanner on to the head of a girl?"

"No, I didn't mean it that specifically . . . oh, very funny. So what now?"

"We split up. You check out the contestants round here, and I'll explore the layout."

"Why do you get to explore?" said Harry.

"Because we're meant to be here to support Dad," Abby said. "It'll look suspicious if we both just leave him. And one of us should keep an eye on him anyway; you know what he's like."

Before Harry could object, Abby disappeared

into the mass of auditionees, many of whom were still discussing whether a ghost would be capable of throwing a spanner.

"Right," said Harry to himself. "Time for some *real* detective work."

CHAPTER 6
Flowers, Toilets and Drivel

Harry scanned the immediate area, wondering who
to target first, when his gaze landed on a woman with
shoulder-length dark brown hair and glasses, heading
through the crowd towards Gus. She was wearing
headphones and holding a clipboard.

He watched as she and Gus had a short conversation.
Then the woman left, looking, Harry thought,
somewhat confused and frustrated.

"What was that about, Dad?" said Harry, walking
over to Gus, who also looked confused.

"I'm not sure," said Gus. "It was very odd. She said
to me, *I know why you're here*. So I said, *Yes, I know why*

I'm here as well. Then she said, *No, I know why you're really here.* I said, *Yes, I know why I'm really here, and I know why're you're really here. You want an autograph, don't you?"*

"Then what happened?" said Harry.

"She just left. Very strange."

"Yes, that is strange," said Harry, who by now had worked out that the woman was the insider, the producer called Josie. "If she comes up to you again, I'd just act as if you know what she's on about."

"Good idea," said Gus. "It wouldn't do to upset my fans, would it?"

"No," said Harry, somewhat gobsmacked by his father's assumption. "So, what you going to do now, Dad?"

"Just sit here and go through my routine, and hope that no other strange people come and talk to me."

"Well, *I'd* better go away then," said Harry, which raised a smile from Gus.

He looked up and reassessed the situation.

"Right," said Harry to himself. "Where was I?"

He looked around. It was still very busy, but he

spotted a seat next to a woman dressed as a flower. Harry didn't think she quite fitted the profile of a criminal mastermind, or someone who wanted to destroy the show, but he wasn't prepared to rule anyone out at this stage, not even a human daffodil.

"Hello," said Harry, plonking himself down next to her. "That was close with the spanner, wasn't it?"

"It was definitely a ghost," said the woman firmly. "I can see them, you know." She leaned in closer to Harry. "They've told me I'm definitely going to win the show."

Harry blinked, looked at the woman/flower and instantly decided he *could* rule her out. She definitely wasn't a mastermind of any sort. The giveaway should have been the daffodil costume.

Sitting the other side of Harry, though, was someone of far more interest to an undercover detective, a young man who was talking in an agitated manner to a woman on the other side of him.

As the daffodil lady told Harry that flower arranging was going to be the next big thing, Harry did his best to listen whilst also straining to hear the man and get a proper look at him.

He was wearing a tuxedo, and had glasses and a moustache, which didn't tell Harry that much. However, when he leaned forward briefly, Harry saw he had GREGOR THE GOBSMACKING written in big, gold, sparkly letters on the back of his jacket, and he also had a wand in one hand. It didn't take much detective work to figure out he was a magician.

"They'd better not reject me again," he was saying in a low, urgent voice. "I'm telling you, there'll be trouble if they do . . . big trouble."

Now this was *definitely* the sort of thing a desperate man potentially out to scupper the show would say. Perhaps, thought Harry, he'd set up the dog video to boost the show's ratings. That way loads of people would see the "trouble" he was planning. And maybe, continued Harry's thought process, he'd also done all those other things, to send a message to the producers that he was serious and not someone to be messed with.

Very carefully Harry reached for the recording device taped to the side of his chest. He undid a button and slipped his hand inside his shirt.

"Of course pansies were very popular last year, but now carnations are all the rage. What are you doing?"

"What do you mean?" said Harry.

"With your hand," said the flower lady.

"Oh, erm, I have an itch."

She nodded knowingly. "That'll be the ectoplasm. From the ghost. It can be very irritating. I've got some cream for that."

As the woman started searching in her floral-patterned bag, Harry saw that the magician was getting up.

"Sorry," he said. "I think some ectoplasm has got into my . . . bottom. Gotta go to the toilet, bye."

Harry jumped up to follow the magician, leaving the flower woman speechless for probably the first time in her life.

Over on the other side of the waiting area, Abby was having her own toilet issues.

"But there's a toilet right there," she was saying to two security guards. "And I'm desperate. Can't I just use that one?"

The security guards shook their heads.

"Sorry, you need a pass to go through to that area," one of them said firmly, a tall, thin man with a squashy nose.

"But I have a pass!" said Abby, waving it frantically. "My dad's a contestant."

The guard glanced at it. "That allows you into the contestants' waiting area and the canteen, but nowhere else unaccompanied. This area is for show staff only."

Abby had already figured that out (the guards were a bit of a giveaway). She knew that the offices and the gallery – the control room where the director and her team worked – were down there, and she had set her sights on getting through to continue her investigations.

"If you haven't got an access-all-areas pass, we can't let you through," said the guard.

"But I might have an accident before I find another toilet," said Abby, crossing her legs and scrunching up her face. "Pleeeaasse?"

The other security guard was a woman. She looked at her colleague and made a face. The man raised his eyebrows. The woman smiled. It was the first time Abby had seen two people have a conversation without using any words.

"Go on then," said the man, stepping aside. "But be quick."

"Thanks," said Abby, bounding through the gap between the guards. "Thanks very much."

She headed in the direction of the toilet, but when she glanced back she saw the guards weren't watching, so she slipped past it and round the corner.

As she'd expected, Abby now found herself in a corridor with various rooms off it marked PRODUCTION OFFICE, GALLERY, SOUND AND LIGHTING. It wasn't quite as busy here, but there were still plenty of people rushing around.

Most of them ignored Abby, but she did get one or two curious glances, so she decided to try and fit in a little more. She got out her phone and pretended to be having an important conversation.

"I see," she said in a serious voice to the person on the other end of the phone, who didn't exist. "Well, I'll have to speak to the producer about that because, erm, those are the sort of things you have to talk to her about."

Despite Abby thinking *I'm talking complete and utter drivel*, her tactic seemed to be working. People stopped paying her attention.

"I'd have to check that with the sound editing supervisory lighting committee," said Abby, gaining confidence. "They might need to reconfigure the edit to achieve optimum edit reconfiguration."

Abby's drivel was getting more drivelly, and she was even thinking that before long the non-existent person on the other end was going to hang up, when suddenly there was a loud bang.

Startled, Abby turned to see a short woman with ginger hair and a furious look on her long, pointy face storming down the corridor. She had clearly just slammed the door of the production office shut, which accounted for the bang, and was striding past everyone, pushing them aside as if she were a rugby player.

Abby nimbly moved out of her way and was considering apologizing to the non-existent person on her phone when she heard another, smaller bang.

The woman's phone had fallen out of her pocket and on to the floor.

Abby picked it up and started to head after her to return it when some text messages caught her eye.

Don't worry, Tanya, I'll be there.

Gr8! No one takes my job and gets away with it!!!

They are really going to regret this!!!

This was very intriguing and Abby was about to take a picture of the messages on her own phone when a voice said, "What are you doing?"

"Oh, nothing, nothing at all," spluttered Abby. "Erm, I was just going to return . . . oh, it's you, Rosy."

"Yes. First aid said I could go," said Rosy. "How come *you're* back here?"

"I needed the toilet, and—"

"WHAT ARE YOU DOING WITH MY PHONE??!!!!"

Abby's heartbeat, which had only just started to come down after being spotted by Rosy, went haywire again. She turned to see the angry woman's furious face about three centimetres from her own. It was almost the same colour as her hair.

"You d-dropped it," said Abby. "I, er, was about to. . ."

"Just give it to me!" snapped Tanya, stepping closer. Her breath smelt strongly of coffee.

Abby nervously held out the phone.

Tanya snatched it and stomped off without so much as a thank you or a ta very much.

"I hope everyone who works on the show isn't like her," said Rosy. "She does *not* seem like a very nice person."

"No," said Abby. "She really doesn't."

CHAPTER 7
Charming!

Harry loved detective programmes. One of his favourite bits was where the detective would follow a suspect.

They always seemed to stay just out of sight of the person they were following whilst skilfully managing to avoid bumping into other people. Harry always thought he'd be really good at it. How difficult could it be?

The answer, it seemed, was *very*.

"Sorry ... excuse me ... sorry... Oops, was that your toe?" were some of the things Harry said as he struggled through the crowd in his pursuit of Gregor, the angry magician.

Inevitably, Harry lost him, so, a little dejected, he made his way back to Gus.

He arrived to find a tall young man in a loud yellow-and-purple-striped jacket vigorously shaking Gus's hand. He had messy straw-blond hair and large ears, which contrasted severely with the rest of his small facial features.

"Thank you so much, Mr Moore," he was saying. "I really, really appreciate it."

"No problem, Nick," said Gus. "Always happy to share my vast experience with an up-and-coming new talent."

The young man backed away, practically bowing as he did so.

"Who was that?" said Harry. "He looks as if he lost a fight with a bucket of very colourful paint."

"Some new comedian, and a fan of course. I gave him a spot of advice. It's always good for us bigger, more successful stars to give something back," said Gus.

Harry waited for Gus's face to break into a smile, but it didn't. He was being serious.

"You do know he's also one of your competitors," said Harry.

"Please, Harry! As if I have worry about someone just starting out," guffawed Gus. "Now, where's the toilet? I need to spend fifteen pennies and a book token."

Harry shook his head. That was another Dad joke he'd heard about three million times before.

"It's over there in the corner," said a voice that sounded a lot like Abby, mainly because it was Abby. "I seem to have found out a lot about toilets today."

"Ah yes," said Gus, getting up and heading off.

"Hi, Agent Abby. Anything to report?" said Harry.

"Ha ha," said Abby, giving him a meaningful look. "Ignore him, Rosy. Harry calls me Agent Abby because I'm so . . . nosy."

Harry, who had just spotted Rosy hovering behind Abby, went pink.

"Ha ha, yes," he said. "And because . . . we both want to be estate agents when we grow up."

Abby made a face at Harry that said a lot of things, but mainly, *Is that the best you can come up with?*

"OK," said Rosy. "I'm going to get a drink. Want anything?"

"No thanks," said Abby. "See you in a minute."

"Sure . . . Agent Abby," said Rosy, grinning a little as she headed off.

"Sorry," said Harry. "Estate agent was the first thing that came into my mind."

"Maybe go for the second thing next time, or even the third. Now listen, I have actually got something to report."

Harry listened intently as Abby told him about Tanya the angry ginger-haired woman and her text messages.

"I don't exactly know what her job was, but clearly someone has taken it and she's not happy," said Abby.

"Hmm, she definitely seems like someone out for revenge. We should investigate her further," Harry said, trying to sound like a real detective.

He was about to tell Abby his news when, not for the first time that day, there was a commotion. And, also not for the first time that day, it involved Gus.

"Why don't you look where you're going!" a woman in a bright orange robe was yelling at Gus. She had long black hair with a thick fringe and glasses.

"I'm sorry," said Gus. "But what do you expect if you bring a basket of dirty washing to a TV show?"

"Dirty washing?!" shouted the woman. "It wasn't dirty washing, you clumsy oaf!"

"Well, what *was* in the basket?!" bellowed Gus back at her.

The woman lowered her voice and said, "My name is Ali. I'm a snake charmer. So what do you *think* was in the basket?"

"Er, a snake?" replied Gus.

"Yes," said Ali, and then, so loudly her glasses fell off, "MY SNAKE!!!!"

If the altercation hadn't already aroused attention, it most certainly did now. The chaos in the room increased tenfold as dancers performed moves they didn't know they had in them and singers hit the highest notes they'd ever hit.

The animals stole the show, though. There was a mash-up of barking, neighing, mooing (that was a very confused dog), whimpering (though that could have been a human) and, yes, squawking – the poor chickens were having the most terrible day.

In amongst it all, Ali was running around looking for her snake.

"Bertie! Bertie!" she called frantically. (Bertie was the snake's name, though it was a Burmese python, so probably not the one its parents had given it.)

The producers and camera crew didn't know what to do, and were quite scared themselves. Only a herd of wildebeest stampeding on a giant trampoline would have come close to the utter carnage unfolding.

"Where's Dad?" shouted Harry over the noise.

"I don't knoooooooooowwwwwwwwwwwwww..." shouted Abby as she was sent flying by a large English sheepdog.

She was wrestling herself up again when Ali shouted, "Got him!" and instantly the room became eerily quiet, as if they'd all been playing musical statues and the music had stopped.

Ali draped Bertie around her neck and made her way through the crowd to his basket. The snake had tan and dark-brown markings and a long head with a tongue that was constantly zipping in and out. Ali had large, welcoming brown eyes and a soft, round, gentle face, yet somehow the two of them seemed well-matched.

Ali put Bertie back in the basket and closed the lid. She seemed much more relaxed now and began playing some calming music on her special snake charmer's pipe, or pungi, probably to send Bertie off into a nice, relaxing sleep. It was very calming, Harry thought, yawning slightly.

"There," Ali said. "Panic over."

And just like that, it was. There were a few murmurs about the incident being another example of the curse at work, but for the most part everything went back to the previous level of chaos, as if nothing had happened (though the odd animal poop and feathers on the floor were evidence to the contrary).

"Hello. Did you drop this?"

Abby turned to see a very tall man, dressed smartly in a suit and waistcoat, holding something out towards her. It was her undercover microphone. It must have come out when she fell over.

"Oh yes, thank you," said Abby. "It's . . . erm, it's. . ."

"Her hearing aid," interjected Harry.

"Yes, that's it," said Abby, taking the microphone. "For my hearing."

"I think he knows what a hearing aid is for," said Harry.

"Yes I do," laughed the man. "There was quite a treasure trove on the floor. I've also just returned a set of false teeth, some earrings and three phones. I found the snake charmer's glasses as well. She was very grateful, said she could hardly see anything without them. I guess she must have used her sense of smell to find the snake. My name's Erran, by the way."

"I'm Abby and this is Harry," said Abby. "We're here with our dad, Gus, who's a comedian. Are you also in the competition?"

"Yes, I'm a hypnotist. Speaking of which" – he glanced behind them – "would you like me to help your friend?"

They turned to look where Erran was gesturing.

Rosy!

They had completely forgotten about her. She must

have walked into the chaos on her way back from the canteen. She was sitting in a chair gripping a can of lemonade so tightly it looked as if it might explode. Her eyes were wide open and she wasn't moving, not even a milli-millimetre.

"What's wrong with her?" said Harry.

"I'd say that she's in a terrified catatonic state because of the snake. But I can get her out of it," said Erran, going over to Rosy.

He knelt in front of her. She didn't seem to know he was there at all, but a few moments later, her eyes closed and her head dropped down to her chest. A little while after that, Erran clicked his fingers and Rosy sat up, wide awake and alert.

"There we go," said Erran. "Back to normal and not afraid of snakes any more."

"That's amazing," said Abby. "Hi, Rosy, how are you feeling?"

"I feel great," said Rosy. She gave Erran a shy smile. "Thank you for using your superpowers to help me."

"It's not a superpower," said Erran, laughing. "It's just hypnotism."

"Hypnotism? Wow," said Rosy. "How did you learn to do that?"

"Erm, well," said Erran sheepishly. "I took an online course."

"That's very interesting," said Rosy. She took out her phone and began typing something.

"What are you doing, Rosy?" asked Harry.

"Well," said Rosy, "I'm going to be a big star one day. Probably a presenter like Uncle Mac, but maybe singing or acting. Or all of them. I never thought of hypnotism, though, so I'm adding it to my How to Become a Big Star file."

"Oh, OK," said Harry.

"You see, I have lots of uncles and aunts," continued Rosy. "My parents actually wanted me to stay with Uncle Michael and Auntie Jane while they were away, but I made sure they left me with Uncle Mac, so I could learn about being on television."

She smiled cheekily, then said, "What's that?"

"Oh," said Abby, suddenly realizing she was still holding the undercover microphone. "That's my hearing aid."

"That's a funny-looking hearing aid," said Rosy.

Harry was about to launch into a completely made up speech about how hearing aid technology had really changed in recent years when, to the twins' immense relief, a timid-looking woman in a badly fitting jumper came over, leading a small child who was crying and trembling like a jelly in an earthquake

"Excuse me," she said to Erran. "Don't want to interrupt, only I saw what you did for that little girl. My Angie, she's only nine, but she's also in a state 'cause of the snake." She nodded at her daughter. "She's got to sing soon, and she'll never be able to if she doesn't calm down."

"No problem," said Erran, kneeling in front of Angie. She was the tiniest little thing, with braces on her teeth and blonde hair tied tightly into bunches that hung down on either side of her.

"It took us three buses to get here today, you know," said the woman. "And buses aren't cheap. Cost us a pretty penny, I don't mind telling you."

"Right," said Abby, wondering just why the woman *was* telling her.

"I'm going to do some more research for my file," said Rosy chirpily. "I'll see you later."

Rosy trotted off, and a short while later Erran had worked his magic and Angie was much calmer.

In fact, for a moment, Abby thought, the whole place seemed quite calm, but just then a door slammed and Tanya, the woman with flame-red hair, came marching in.

"Look," whispered Abby, nudging Harry. "That's her. The angry woman who dropped her phone."

Tanya's small body was charged with energy and her hair and face seemed ablaze. If anything, Abby thought she looked even angrier than she had before – and that was saying something.

CHAPTER 8

*The Cat (Not the Snake)
Is Out of the Bag*

Tanya's face was contorted with rage, but, as Abby watched, she took a deep breath and seemed to make a real effort to control her anger. The next moment her expression was radiant and pleasant.

"Could I have everyone's attention, please?" she called.

The noise in the room rippled down to a gentle hubbub of light chatter, and everyone turned to face Tanya.

"Thank you. I'm Tanya, the deputy senior producer. Our new *senior* producer, Josie," she went on through gritted teeth, as if each word was causing her pain, "would like to have a word with you all."

Hundreds of eyes instantly shifted to a woman by her side. She had bright green eyes and a wide mouth, which was made more prominent by red lipstick. Harry recognized her as the secret service insider who had spoken to Gus.

Senior producer, he thought. *I never realized she was so important.*

"Thank you, Tanya," said Josie, in a thick Scottish accent. "I wanted to welcome you all to *Britain's Biggest New Star* – the winner of which is in this room, right now!"

A buzz of excitement shot round the assembled contestants.

"Told you I'd win," said the daffodil lady, to no one in particular.

"But the most important thing," Josie went on, "is for you to have fun today. As far as we're concerned, you're all stars already, so give yourselves a huge round of applause."

Everyone clapped and whooped as if they were one big happy family, albeit quite a dysfunctional one.

"Now then," said Josie. "The show will be starting in fifteen minutes, so please make your final preparations and get ready to take to the stage!"

The gentle hubbub of light chatter instantly rose to a blustery storm of nervous excitement.

"Erm, excuse me."

Josie, who had started to leave, stopped and turned back round.

"Yes?" she said, craning to see who had spoken.

A man wearing a cream-coloured onesie stepped forward a little uncertainly.

"Hello, I'm, er, Lincoln," he said. "I'm a mime artist, but I do talk when I'm not miming."

The room was now completely silent. Lincoln smiled nervously.

"Yes, Lincoln?" said Josie. "What can I do for you?"

"Well, I just wondered, you know ... about the curse."

There was a murmur of agreement from the crowd.

"The curse?" asked Josie, sweetly.

"Yes, there was that video, and a couple of strange things have happened already today, so. . ."

Josie left Lincoln's words hanging in the air for a couple of seconds before answering.

"Thank you, Lincoln, that is a very fair question," said Josie. "So, I may be new, but many of my colleagues have worked on this show for years. And from what they tell me, strange things are always happening in this madhouse." She grinned. "Isn't that right?"

The other producers and show staff around the room all laughed and nodded enthusiastically.

"And so far," continued Josie, "they haven't discovered any cursed ghosts responsible for any of it. However, I know many of you have concerns, so my team have been given instructions to be extra alert. Right, guys?"

"Right!" chorused the other producers.

"So, I suggest you all focus on your performances, because now. . ." She glanced at her watch. "It's only thirteen minutes to showtime."

The room instantly burst into life again.

"You know Josie's the insider," said Harry. "She talked to Dad earlier. It didn't go too well."

Abby nodded. She could imagine.

"So, have *you* got anything to report?" she said.

"Actually, yes," said Harry. He took out his phone and pulled up a clip.

"What's this?" said Abby. The clip was of a young man in a white suit, doing some pretty average magic.

"It's *BBNS*, four series ago. That's a magician called Gregor the Great. He didn't make it past the first show."

"Why are you showing me this?" said Abby.

"Because he's back," said Harry. "And he's pretty angry. He's now called Gregor the Gobsmacking. I overheard him talking to someone. He really didn't like being rejected four years ago, and from what he said, if it happens again, he's planning something pretty bad."

"Good work," said Abby. "Let's both try and keep an eye out for him."

As she spoke, Abby noticed that Rosy had returned and was speaking to Tanya. It was a short conversation, and a couple of minutes later Tanya headed off, texting furiously on her phone as she did so. Abby nudged Harry and they went over.

"What was that about, Rosy?" Harry said, trying to sound as breezy and casual as he could.

"She said I could watch the show in Uncle Mac's dressing room," said Rosy.

"That's nice of him," said Abby.

"Hey, why don't you two come with and we can watch it together?" said Rosy. "I'm sure we'll be safe from the curse and there's some really cool stuff in there."

"We'd love to, but we've got to make sure our dad gets onstage without releasing any more animals or getting into some other trouble," said Harry. "But we'll see you after."

"Great," said Rosy calmly. "So you can tell me your secret then."

"Our secret?" said the twins together. "We haven't got a secret."

Rosy narrowed her eyes and looked at them thoughtfully.

"Well," she said. "*Something* is going on. You were in the staff area, Abby, and you have a very strange hearing aid. And you called each other agent. Plus I told you my secret about me becoming a big star."

The twins were silent. This was bad. Harry and Abby's cover had been blown. By a ten-year-old!

"Please," she said. "This is my uncle's show. If something's wrong, I want to know."

Harry and Abby looked at each other, unsure whether to confess or make up a lie.

"OK," said Harry at last. "There is ... something, but we need to discuss it first. We'll let you know what we've decided after the show."

Rosy beamed.

"OK," she said sweetly. "Me and Teddy will see you then. Bye."

Rosy trotted off happily, allowing the twins to breathe normally for the first time in a little while.

"I do think we should tell her what we're doing here," said Harry. "She's Mac's niece. She might be useful. She's also been almost decapitated by a spanner and scared out of her mind by a snake, so it's not been the best day for her so far."

"OK," said Abby. "But we have to be more careful from now on. If Rosy can suss us out, I'm sure it wouldn't be too difficult for the real criminal."

"Fine. So what now?" said Harry.

"Well, one of us needs to make sure Dad gets

onstage at the right time. And one of us needs to keep an eye on the other contestants and producers. If the criminal is planning anything, now is the time for them to go into action."

"OK," said Harry. "But I've done a lot of staying with Dad, so I'll do it till the show starts, but then it's your turn. I want to sit in the audience. There's another few thousand potential suspects out there, and if any of them try anything, I'm going to pounce!"

"You mean, you'll contact Trevor, and he'll get his *team* to pounce," Abby reminded him.

"Yes, that's exactly what I meant," said Harry. "Now off you go and try not to lose your hearing aid."

CHAPTER 9

Hypnotic Interference

With thirteen minutes and counting to showtime, Abby wasn't entirely sure what to do with herself. There was just so much going on in the waiting area that in the unlikely event of her growing four extra heads, she'd still have had trouble keeping an eye on it all.

Thankfully, she didn't need to look far to see something very interesting indeed.

Over in a corner was Erran, the hypnotist. He was so tall that he was something of a lighthouse in this ocean of humanity – and Abby could see that he was having quite an intense conversation with someone. And that someone only happened to be Tom, the handyman, who had apparently "dropped" the spanner earlier.

As Abby watched, she was certain she saw Tom slip something into Erran's hand.

She couldn't see what it was, but she *could* see that Tom was clearly nervous. He kept looking around anxiously as Erran was talking.

The two of them then headed off in different directions.

Keeping her distance, Abby followed Erran. She turned out to be much better at it than her brother, working her way seamlessly through the crowd until she saw him approach the staff area.

Abby stopped and watched as Erran walked up, flashed a pass at the security guards and went through.

They'd told her that contestants didn't have passes to that area. But a handyman would. Tom must have given Erran an access-all-areas pass!

The question was – why?

Abby decided to find out.

"Hi," she said cheerily, approaching the guards. "Me again. Desperate for the toilet, remember?"

The two of them looked at each other and shook their heads.

"You're not going to believe this, but silly me's just drunk a big glass of water, huge actually, because it's so hot in here, and now I, er, need to go again. Badly. So could I . . . ?"

"No," said the woman.

"No," said the man.

"But you let me through before and I'm even more desperate this time," pleaded Abby.

"No," they both said together with a firmness that implied, *If you ask again, you might want to consider making a will.*

Abby sighed and turned away. Despite the disappointment, her mind was buzzing as she made her way back to Harry and Gus. Erran seemed like a nice guy. Why did he need to get into the off-limits staff area? Had he hypnotized Tom to get his pass *and* to drop the spanner, or were they in this together? But if so, why would Erran want to sabotage the show?

"Hey," said Harry as Abby pitched up. It was less busy in the waiting area now, as some contestants had been taken through to the side of the stage, ready to go on. "Anything to report?"

"Only Tom giving Erran a pass to the staff area," she said. "Why would he want to get back there?"

"Who knows? Maybe lots of the staff are also terrified of snakes and he's gone to help them. Or it could be something far more sinister," Harry said. "Definitely suspicious, though. Good work."

"How's Dad been?" said Abby.

"Like a little lamb," said Harry. "He's been going through his set. It's good, I think the audience are going to like it."

"Let's hope so," said Abby. "It would be terrible if he didn't make it through this round."

"But that's not going to happen," said Harry. "Trevor and Josie must have a plan B."

Abby shrugged. Neither of them knew what, if any, plans had been made in that respect.

"Anyway, he's got to stay here until he's called, so it's over to you now. Don't let him wander off," said Harry. "I'm going to sit in the audience, the show is about to start."

Harry hurriedly made his way through to the stage area. The audience were mostly seated in rows, but there were also two small mosh pits on either side of the stage full of very excited people jumping around and dancing.

When he arrived, Harry found the audience being whipped into a frenzy by Stuart the warm-up man, whose job was to get them even more excited than they already were.

This was so that when the show started, they would scream, shout and applaud like children who had eaten an awful lot of sweets. In that respect, Harry could see that Stuart was doing very well.

He had everyone standing up, dancing and singing to "We Are the Champions" by Queen. He'd also split the audience into two teams who were competing to be the loudest. As the contest ended, Harry slipped into a seat near the back.

"OK," said Stuart, gesturing for everyone to sit down as the music stopped. "I think the winners that time were ... this side of the audience!"

The winning side erupted in celebration, whilst the

other side booed and jeered in mock disappointment. Harry could already feel his ears ringing.

"OK, we're going to start the live show very soon," said Stuart, "but before we do, please make sure your phones are turned off. And that means *off*; they can still affect our equipment on silent. Thank you."

The few people who had forgotten to do so turned their phones off, which included Harry.

"Right, are you ready to meet your host?" boomed Stuart.

The audience could hardly have been *more* ready and let Stuart know in no uncertain terms.

"Then please welcome unquestionably the most talented and handsome man in Britain, Mr Mac Tatum!"

The audience roared again as Mac strode out on to the stage, bear-hugged Stuart and bowed graciously to the audience.

"Thank you," said Mac. "You lot are fantastic, by far the best audience we've had today."

Everyone in the studio howled with laughter at a joke Mac had probably made three thousand times before.

As the laughter subsided, Harry remembered that he wasn't just there to watch the show; he had a job to do.

Now what would a great detective do in this situation? he asked himself.

The answer was probably to sit tight, blend into the crowd and stay alert. However, Harry thought that sounded boring, so instead he accidentally on purpose dropped a pen, so he could duck down and look under the seats for anything untoward. All he saw were legs, a few bags and some chewing gum, which was all very toward, if that is the opposite of untoward.

Sitting up, he surveyed the scene, but all he could see were excited people enjoying themselves. There wasn't a sniff of anything suspicious.

"Right, I've got to nip backstage now," Mac was saying. "We go live in thirty seconds. Have a great show, everyone."

"Mac Tatum, ladies and gentlemen!" roared Stuart as Mac scurried off. "And remember, when he next comes on, you lot need to go *ballistic*. Can you do that for me?"

The audience seemed very sure of their capabilities in that respect and, as one, shouted "Yes!" back at Stuart.

The lights went down and a hush laced with anticipation descended.

Moments later, a voice boomed through the studio.

"People get ready. The search is on for Britain's Biggest New Star! Now, please welcome your host, Mr Mac Tatum!"

Right on cue, the audience duly went ballistic, and also bananas, bonkers, berserk and barmy for good measure.

The show had begun.

CHAPTER 10

The Show Must Go On

"You feeling OK, Dad?"

Gus smiled absently and gave Abby a thumbs up. Then he went back to rehearsing his lines.

Abby looked around. The atmosphere in the waiting area was now tense and subdued as everyone nervously watched the show on the various screens dotted about the place and waited to be called.

Tom was nowhere to be seen, but Erran was there, looking cheerful and pretty relaxed. Gregor, the angry magician, was pacing silently back and forth, occasionally glancing at the screens, and Ali was sitting with Bertie's basket in her lap, her hands resting firmly on the top.

"Not the toilet again! You'll wear those shoes out and they cost a fortune!"

Abby glanced over to see Angie and her mum heading to the loo. The poor girl seemed very nervous and Abby wondered how she would manage onstage in front of all those people.

They disappeared in to the ladies' just as Nick, the young comedian who had been chatting to Gus, came out of the gents'. His colourful jacket was probably the loudest thing in the room.

Even the animals were quiet. There wasn't a peep from the chickens, and the eight members of a doggy dance troupe called Hot Dogs seemed positively bored, though their owner and dance leader, Roisin, was biting her nails.

Abby sighed and looked up. A big opening performance by a new boy band filled the screen. It looked fantastic and Abby felt a pang of jealousy. Harry was probably having a great time in the audience.

A moment later, though, she felt a pang of something very different as she caught a glint of cold, hard steel.

A knife!

Someone had a knife!

Abby swung round, her finger resting on the microphone, ready to alert Trevor and his team.

A word from her, she imagined, and the place would be swarming with crack agents ready to disarm the most vicious of criminals. It was quite lucky, therefore, that she didn't alert Trevor.

It *was* a knife. But the knife belonged to a knife thrower called Blade. In fact, he had ten, all for his act.

Shaking her head, Abby wondered whether the whole curse thing *was* just some crank ex-contestant who had made their point. Perhaps she and Harry were wasting their time.

She needn't have worried. Things were about to get very interesting indeed. . .

"One more time, give it up for the hottest band around – Upload!"

Harry and the rest of the audience cheered as the four members of the boy band waved and glided offstage.

"OK, our first contestant is coming up very soon," Mac said. "But first it's time to welcome Cheddar, Stilton,

Camembert and Brie ... otherwise known as the four biggest cheeses in the business ... it's our judges!!!"

Pandemonium ensued as Diamond, Eve, Wally and Clive appeared and assembled in a line in the middle of the stage.

"Diamond!" hollered Mac.

The audience cheered and then went quiet. They knew what was coming. Diamond, whose vocal range was as well-known as her diva-ish ways, was famous for singing a long note whenever she was introduced, and tonight, it was a very high one.

"Laaaaaaaaaaaaaaaaaaaaaaaa!"

The audience roared as she finished and bowed deeply. She was the youngest judge, with five double-platinum albums to her name, and radiated glamour in a sequinned gown.

"Clive Derek!" boomed Mac.

Funnyman Clive had clearly spent some time with the hair and make-up team. He now looked beautifully coiffured and clean shaven, and was wearing a dark designer suit. He always went for a laugh and this time he saluted the audience, "accidentally" poking himself in the eye while doing so. They loved it.

"Eve Cotton!" yelled Mac.

Eve had been a big soap star some years ago, but her acting career faltered after that. When reality TV came calling, she jumped at the chance and won a couple of big shows, which kept her in the limelight enough to get the call to be on the judging panel for *BBNS*. Tonight she'd dyed her blonde locks black and was wearing a leather jumpsuit.

She loved playing up to the audience, so when her name was called, she pretended to be surprised and made a big *Who, me?* face. Then she twirled around, returning to face the front with a huge smile as she applauded the audience herself.

"And finally, the big man himself – Wally Deighton!" shouted Mac.

Wally was older than the others, in his sixties. He'd created and owned the show and was therefore the unofficial head judge. He wore a well-cut blue suit and looked relaxed. He'd been in "the business" as a talent agent for years, signing some of the biggest names from the last few decades, and everyone respected him.

He liked to play it cool so just tapped a forefinger to his head and smiled confidently.

"Our judges, everyone!" Mac said again, which was the cue for them to make their way down some steps and towards a desk facing the stage.

From where he was sitting, Harry craned his neck to get a better look at them. If they were in any way worried about the curse, he thought, they certainly weren't showing it. They seemed to be the most relaxed people in the room.

"There they go," said Mac. "The biggest stars on the planet . . . and Clive Derek. Love you, Clive."

The audience laughed as Clive turned and shouted, "Love you too, Mac."

"Right, time to get serious," continued Mac as the noise subsided. "We are on the hunt for Britain's Biggest New Star. From the thousands who applied, thirty acts have made it this far, but only one of them can win that life-changing prize. So let's—"

BBBBBBBRRRRRUUUUPPPPPPPPPHHHHHHHT TTTTTFFFFFFLLLLLLLUUUUUUUUPPPPPPPPPP PFFFFFFF!

Mac stopped. He'd been interrupted when speaking many times before, but never by the sound of an enormous fart. Or rather, FOUR enormous farts, unleashed simultaneously on the unsuspecting audience.

For a moment there was silence as people tried to figure out what had just happened. Then Clive stood up, holding a whoopee cushion aloft.

The reaction was incredible. There was hysteria. People were crying with laughter.

And it *was* hilarious. But sitting in the audience, Harry knew that something wasn't right. Mac seemed completely thrown by what had happened. Diamond looked embarrassed, Eve shocked and Wally was downright angry and, as Harry could see, he was staring daggers at a producer standing out of shot to his left.

In the contestants' waiting area there had also been howls of laughter, but only from the contestants and their families. As Abby noted, the production staff there were all looking at each other and shrugging. Clearly, Abby thought, they'd had no idea the whoopee cushion gag was going to happen. So how had it?

As the laughter subsided Clive pulled himself together first.

"Phew!" he said, waving his hand in front of his nose. "I knew we shouldn't have had beans for lunch."

The audience roared again, which seemed to jolt Mac out of his bemusement. He laughed heartily.

"Four hours' rehearsal for that, but I think it was worth it," he said. "Let's hope our judges use their mouths to do the talking from now on."

The judges had also regained their composure now and, having removed the whoopee cushions, all sat down quietly.

"OK, let's crack on with tonight's first act," said Mac. "They're a husband and wife juggling team, so I imagine at their wedding they promised to love, honour and catch everything they throw at each other. This is Colin and Sarah Milligan."

A film of the couple practising in their house played out on the big screen above the stage, but Harry didn't watch it. He kept his eyes firmly on the judges. Now that the viewers at home couldn't see them, a small army of hair and make-up people were furiously prodding, poking, dabbing, scraping and wiping them to make sure not a hair or skin follicle was out of place.

Three seconds before the film ended, the hair and make-up people slipped away and the freshly preened judges sat upright to watch the act.

Harry thought the juggling couple seemed confident as they walked out on to the stage, and he liked their performance, but the judges were clearly still a bit grumpy about the whoopee cushions and gave them four no's.

The next act was Nick, the comedian who had been chatting to Gus. His routine started well, but after about thirty seconds, both Harry's and Abby's ears pricked up considerably.

"I was a strange child – well, no one with a jacket like this can have had a normal childhood, can they? It was actually inspired by my best friend growing up, Farley Crumplewith Binglinton the Third. He was a butterfly. We had great times together. But I did used to wonder . . . if there were butterflies, why weren't there *margarine*-flies? And if there were, would they be softer than butterflies, but not as tasty? Not that I ever ate a butterfly . . . though I did once find half a caterpillar in an apple . . . that was the last time the two of us played hide-and-seek together."

There was a roar of laughter from the crowd.

"Dad," shouted Abby. "Are you listening to this?"

"What?" said Gus, blinking. "No, I was, erm, well, I'm not sure what I was doing, to be honest."

"That comedian has just done some material that sounded an awful lot like your material. Your *new* material!"

"Don't be ridiculous," said Gus, suddenly sitting up and concentrating on the screen.

Sure enough, as Nick continued, there were at least three gags that sounded very similar to ones Gus had planned to do. And they were getting big laughs.

"You didn't tell him any of your jokes, did you, Dad?"

"Of course not," said Gus. "I just gave him advice. It must be a coincidence. It happens sometimes."

"Right," said Abby, who wasn't so sure it was a coincidence. "Well, you can't do the same routine. What are you going to do?"

"Don't worry," said Gus, a bit too breezily for Abby's

liking. "I've got some backup stuff. I just need to learn it."

Gus took out his phone and began searching through his notes. He even started chuckling at some of his own jokes.

Abby continued watching the comedian. Stealing someone else's material didn't mean Nick was the one sabotaging the show – but it *did* make him untrustworthy. Abby thought it was definitely worth keeping an eye on Nick Lanston.

Whilst Abby was mulling that over, Harry was in the audience, fuming. Not only had the comedian stolen Gus's material, but the judges loved his act and put him through to the next round.

A moment later, though, Harry found himself in the middle of a screaming mob. Mac had just announced that the young singer Angie Potter was up next, and it appeared Harry was sitting right in amongst her family.

"That's my daughter," said the man next to him, in between whoops and screams.

The film about Angie started to play and before long the whole audience fell silent.

Angie's short life had been tough. The family didn't have much and had really struggled. At the end Angie said that *BBNS* was a chance for her to change not just her life, but her whole family's life.

The film finished and Angie came out. The audience, most of whom were in tears, cheered loudly.

"Can't believe it," said Angie's dad. "My girl up there. It's amazing."

Angie seemed even tinier onstage in her orange dress. She looked like a lonely tangerine segment that wanted nothing more than to rejoin its friends and snuggle back beneath the peel.

"Angie, sweetheart," said Eve. "You look gorgeous, really. Tell us, if you did win the show, what's the first thing you'd do?"

It took Angie a few seconds to answer; she seemed completely overawed.

"I . . . I would take Mum and Dad to Pizza Palace for the biggest pizza ever. They love pizza, but we haven't been there for ages. We can't afford it."

The audience "aaaahed", and Eve clasped her hands

to her heart.

"That's beautiful," she said. "I really hope you do well."

"Good luck," Harry whispered to Angie's dad.

"Thanks, mate," he said quietly, and then a moment later he stood up, punched the air with his fist and hollered, "Go on, Ang, you can do it!"

Harry ears were ringing a little after that, but as the man sat down, Harry noticed that the sleeve of his jacket had ridden up along his arm, revealing what seemed to be a very expensive-looking watch. A Rolex, no less. It didn't quite fit with someone who had very little, thought Harry.

Of course, it could have been a cheap fake, but Harry didn't want Abby to think he'd forgotten about his undercover work. She was probably finding loads of clues and suspects, so at least this was something he could report back about.

Harry was wondering how to take a picture of the Rolex without anyone noticing when Angie's dad shot up again. In fact, just about everyone was now on their feet.

Angie had started singing and while her voice was OK, thought Harry, she wasn't amazing. The audience were all on her side, though, and they stood and danced along as she sang.

Angie's dad, in particular, was transfixed on his daughter, which gave Harry the chance to switch on his phone and carefully take as many pictures as he could. Surely there'd be one good one of the Rolex.

Angie finished and a roar went up like a mighty ocean of approval. It was quite clear people loved her and if any of the judges disagreed, that would NOT go down well.

But the judges loved her too. They talked about Angie as if she was the most talented nine-year-old on the planet, and she waltzed through to the next round with four yesses.

"Incredible," said Mac, as Angie walked off. "When I was nine I thought tying my own shoelaces was a great achievement ... which it was. I wore slip-ons. Right, don't go anywhere, there's plenty more to come after the break. We'll see you soon!"

CHAPTER 11

A Shot in the Dark

"That's the first time we've ever had a snake charmer on the show, so you could say that HISSSSStory has been made!"

Mac paused for laughter. There wasn't any.

"The judges loved it so we'll be seeing them again in the next round. Give it up for Ali Saperas and Bertie!"

Abby watched on the television screen nearest to her as Ali, with Bertie the snake around her neck, waved to the audience and headed offstage.

Abby had enjoyed watching the performance, but the truth was, she was restless. There was still nothing much to interest anyone where she was in the waiting area, and certainly not a spy.

She stood up and stretched.

"I'm going for a walk, Dad," she said.

"Sure," said Gus. She knew he wasn't paying much attention – he was too busy practising his routine, but he looked cheerful. Abby really hoped he knew what he was letting himself in for.

Abby headed to the canteen. It had been pretty busy in there, but now the show was on, it was quiet. The only people in there were a group of smart-looking types sitting in front of computers. Abby sauntered over.

"Hi," she said.

"Hi," said one of them, not looking up from her screen.

"Do you mind if I ask what you're doing?" said Abby innocently.

"We're the online team," said the girl, still not looking up. "We update the show's social media and website, and monitor the reaction." Then, ignoring Abby, she turned to the person next to her. "Look, here's another one." She started reading the tweet on her screen. "Mac's behind it all. He knows he's going to be fired at the end of the series because of low ratings. He wants to take the show down and go out in a blaze of glory."

"How many's that now?" said one of the others.

"Quite a few," said the girl. "I'd say this theory is pretty widespread."

Abby moved away and sat down at a nearby table. Ratings *had* been bad for the previous series, she thought. Was Mac really going to be fired, and did he know that? If so...

Her train of thought was broken when Angie and her family came in. They were carrying a big bottle of champagne and a huge box of chocolates.

"Congratulations, Angie," Abby said. "Nice of the show to give you chocolates!"

"Yeah, it was," said her dad, before Angie could say anything. "Real nice. Oh look, there's that snake charmer with a film crew. Probably going to do her backstage shots. We've just done that, it was great."

Abby turned to see Ali enter, followed by a camera

operator and producer. They set up in the corner of the canteen.

"OK, Ali," said the producer. "Call your mum and tell her you got through. And don't worry about us, just act as if we're not here."

Obediently, Ali rang her mum. Before long there were excited squeals from both of them.

"That was great, Ali," said the producer. "But could you do it again, please, and this time be, like, *really* excited and happy?"

Ali looked surprised – she *was really* excited – but she did it again, doubling her efforts and oozing happiness from every pore of her body.

"Fantastic. Thanks, Ali," said the producer, scurrying off to find another contestant to interview.

Abby shook her head and was about to congratulate Ali on her performance when she realized that Ali was still on the phone.

"Yes, they've gone now, Mum," said Ali. "And yes," she continued, lowering her voice, "the plan is working. I haven't been recognized."

Abby felt a surge of nervous excitement. The plan?

What was that about? She worked with snakes, for goodness' sake. The potential for sabotage was *huge* – it had been bad enough when Bertie had escaped. Maybe she was planning to release hundreds next time, and on live television! Maybe the royal family were all secretly terrified of snakes?

Either way, thought Abby as she headed back to Gus, Ali needed some serious investigation.

"Our next act," Mac was saying onstage, "is a lady with a lot of power . . . *flower* power. From Rotherham, it's the blooming marvellous Daisy Lily!"

Daisy Lily was the daffodil lady. Harry leaned forward. This he had to see.

Her act, which just involved dancing, badly, whilst putting flowers in a vase, got an understandably lukewarm response from the audience. Clive, who had championed her audition tape and been largely responsible for putting her through to the live shows, loved her, though, and gave her a yes.

"Come on, it's genius," said Clive, cajoling the other three judges. "I'm sure she'll really blossom in the next round."

"Daisy, you know I love you," said Eve. "You're a beautiful flower yourself, but it's not quite what we're looking for, so I'm afraid it's a no from me."

Diamond was next. "This is so tough," she said. "You've made a gorgeous bouquet there, it's like a song made out of petals. You know what? I want to see what you do next, so I'm going to say yes."

That made it two yesses to one no. Three yesses was enough to get through to the next round, so everything rested on Wally's decision. It was almost as if they'd planned it that way to increase the tension.

Wally, however, was a very forthright, no-nonsense person. When it came to decision making, he didn't beat about the bush.

"Sorry, Daisy," he said. "You're a very nice lady, but your act is not for me. It's a no."

Daisy looked pretty dejected but walked offstage to generous applause.

A street dance troupe and a pianist were the next two acts. Their performances went well, and Harry was starting to relax and enjoy himself. *The whoopee cushions were just a practical joke*, he thought. *It doesn't seem as if anyone is out to sabotage the show tonight.*

He was about to be proved very wrong.

The next act was a BMX bike acrobatics team. Harry loved them. They did all the tricks: 360s, barspins, nose pivots, backflips and more. It was amazing and as the performance reached its finale, Harry wondered what they were going to do for their big ending.

He watched open-mouthed as the riders all lined up on one side of the stage. Then they took off and were mid-way across the stage when a trapdoor in the floor suddenly opened.

Harry, and the rest of the audience, gasped. Two of the bikes were heading directly for it. Incredibly, the riders were so good, they were able to take off and fly over the hole, and, as a stagehand rushed out to shut the door, the whole team managed to finish the routine.

The audience gave them a standing ovation, but as they stood listening to the judges' comments, Harry could tell they were really shaken. The trapdoor opening had definitely not been planned.

The judges praised them enormously, though, and

they sailed, or rather, cycled, through to the next round.

"Amazing," said Mac as the bikers exited the stage. "And apologies for the little accident there. Just one of the perils of live television."

Hmm, thought Harry. *That "accident" could have been deadly.*

And that was only the beginning.

There was another "little accident" during the Hot Dogs' performance. As the dogs were walking on their hind legs to classical music, the sprinklers over the stage went off.

The dogs were drenched and ran off, shaking themselves dry all over the judges. The audience thought it was hilarious, but the judges, whose hair and make-up teams had to work superfast in the break, were *not* amused.

Up next were a girl group, Girly Wirly, an acrobatic trio and Lincoln the mime artist, who all got through, and a lady who made it look as if her painted toenails were singing, who didn't. They all passed off without incident.

Then Mac introduced the next performance.

"OK, up next, a lovely guy, but I wouldn't invite him round for dinner. You might find you have less cutlery afterwards – *and* a couple of missing fingers.

"Seriously, though, what you're about to see takes years of practice, so please don't try this at home. Hoping he makes the *cut* for the next round, it's our amazing knife thrower, Blade!"

Blade's film played and then he strode out onstage in a shiny silver jumpsuit, which reflected the studio lights, sending bright shards out above the audience's heads.

As soon as he reached the centre of the stage, he spun round and fired four knives into four watermelons perched on stands behind him.

Next, he threw three knives up in to the air and stood still as they plunged into the floor, missing him by millimetres.

The audience gasped and went into rapturous applause. More astonishing feats of accuracy and bravery followed before his big finale.

Blade looked out across the audience. "For the final and most dangerous part of my act," he said, "I need the help of someone strong and fearless, with nerves of steel. Diamond, I think that might be you."

The audience chuckled. Diamond could be feisty but she was famously scared of everything under the sun.

"I ... I'm really not sure about this," she said, stepping nervously on to the stage.

"You have nothing to fear," said Blade, strapping her on to a large, spinning circle.

"Whatever you do," said Diamond nervously, "please don't shut your eyes."

Blade grinned. "OK, I won't," he said. "How about I do this instead?"

He took a blindfold out of his pocket and put it on.

"No way!" shouted Diamond. "No. Way."

The wheel started spinning and Blade threw the first of six knives he was holding. It missed Diamond's right knee by the narrowest of margins. The next four also landed centimetres from her body, embedding themselves into the wooden circle with a terrifying SHTUNKKKKK!

Now he only had one knife left. Holding it aloft, Blade slowly turned around. He was not only blindfolded now, he was also facing the wrong way.

The audience held their breath, Harry included. It was as if they were all sitting together on the edge of one enormous seat.

Blade stretched out his arm and then lifted it up and over his shoulder, so that the point of the knife was facing the circle. He brought it down again and then lifted it up once more. He brought it down a third time and just as he released the knife...

DARKNESS. COMPLETE AND UTTER DARKNESS.

The lights had gone out.

There was a moment of stunned silence, and then the screams rang out, the loudest of which came from Diamond.

A couple of seconds later the lights came on again. Everyone blinked as their eyes adjusted, then turned to look at the stage.

The sixth knife was there, embedded just above Diamond's head.

Confused applause broke out. Some of the audience

clearly thought it was part of the act. But Harry was pretty sure they were wrong.

Blade had taken the blindfold off and looked horrified. Diamond, who had been helped off the circle, was shaking. The other judges were staring with their mouths open.

As Harry scanned the stage, he spotted Mac seemingly having a very animated conversation with himself. He wasn't; he was actually speaking to Josie via an earpiece, and he looked very serious and concerned.

As the camera panned back to him, he forced a smile.

"Well," he said to Blade. "That was quite something!"

"I ... I ... it wasn't meant to..." said Blade, still looking shocked.

"Of course it wasn't," said Mac, winking at the camera knowingly. "I think we'll leave Diamond to recover, she'll probably only need six months. What did the rest of our judges make of that, I wonder? Wally?"

The three remaining judges pulled themselves together and spluttered through their comments before putting Blade in to the next round.

"Congratulations," said Mac. "Can't wait to see what you'll do in the next round. Assuming I can see it, of course. One more time, Blade!"

The audience applauded, but as the noise died down, a woman in the audience stood up and shouted, "It was the curse! It's real! The show is cursed!"

There was an anxious murmuring in the audience.

Mac laughed uneasily. "Well, thank you for that comment," he said. "But how many times have I told you about interrupting me on television, Mother?"

That got a laugh from some of the audience, but the damage was done, and as Harry looked around he could hear the rumours fizzing around haphazardly, like balloons emptying of air.

CHAPTER 12

Just a (Back)Stage He's Going Through

"Come in, Agent 4905-3! Are you there?"

After the drama of Diamond's near death experience, Abby was trying to check in with Trevor, but he wasn't answering.

"Where is he?" she muttered. "He can't be having *another* tea break."

Just then, there was a crackle on the other end of the line. "Yes," Trevor said, sounding ratty. "What is it?"

"Are you watching the show?"

"I was *trying* to but you just interrupted me! It's brilliant! That stunt with the lights going off! Amazing!"

"Stunt?" said Abby. "Everyone looked really shocked. That wasn't planned."

"Of course it was planned," said Trevor nonchalantly. "Honestly, Abby, you're so naïve. Oooh, look, the hypnotist is coming on. Bye for now. I mean, over and out."

Abby sighed. She was fit to burst with all the thoughts going round her head and was desperate to speak to Harry and plan their next move. That would have to wait, though.

On the monitor, she saw that Erran the hypnotist was about to start his performance. He was dressed casually in just jeans and a T-shirt, and seemed very calm and in control. Abby watched as he hypnotized audience members. He made one person gurgle like a baby and another believe they were a tree who screamed every time a leaf fell off. It really was very funny and pretty incredible.

Then Erran turned to the judges.

"Now," he said. "I'm told one of our judges has a secret side. A side which you could say is their true *animal nature*. Isn't that right, Eve?"

As soon as Erran said her name, Eve stood up and started hopping around near the judges' table, going, "Ribbit, ribbit, ribbit."

She seemed to have become a frog.

It was hilarious, and made even funnier by the fact that her hair flew up and down as she leapt around.

"Wow, you're really channelling your inner amphibian there," said Erran. "Oh, look, I see a fly, Eve."

Eve's tongue started darting in and out of her mouth as she attempted to catch the non-existent fly.

The audience erupted with laughter again. Erran brought Eve out of her froggy trance, after which she, along with the other judges, gave him four yesses. He left with applause ringing around the studio.

Abby frowned as she watched Erran leave the stage. Hypnotism was a powerful skill, and Erran was clearly very good at it. Erran *could* have hypnotized someone into turning the lights off during Blade's performance. But if so, why? He was doing well on the show – there was no reason for him to scupper it. At least, no reason that anyone had discovered yet...

"Gus Moore?"

Abby looked up. Mikey was standing by the door, holding a clipboard.

"Over here," Gus shouted.

"Great," said Mikey. "Come with me. You're on soon."

"Can I come?" said Abby.

"I don't see why not," said Gus. "Is that OK? She won't be a problem, she's potty trained."

Abby cringed at Gus's joke.

"Sure," Mikey said. "We need to get a move on, though."

They hurried past the security guards – Abby couldn't help smirking as she did so – and into the corridor where the gallery and other rooms were.

At the far end was a door which led into a technical area. They went in and Abby could see lots of people doing things with expensive-looking equipment.

"I'm sorry, excuse me," she said as she squeezed past a man and a woman sitting at a large console full of buttons and sliders. Neither of them heard her, though. They were too deeply embroiled in their own conversation.

"What was Dave thinking?" the woman was saying. "Diamond could have been killed."

"He feels terrible," said the man. "But he swears blind that *Josie* told him to turn the lights off. *And* apparently she told Karen to open the trapdoor and put those whoopee cushions on the judges' chairs."

The woman shook her head. "But that doesn't make sense," she said. "Why would she do that? She's only just got the top job. . ."

Abby was intrigued, but she saw Mikey waving impatiently from the other end of the room and scuttled after him. Coming out of the technical area, Abby found herself at the back of the audience. Now she got a real sense of the buzz and excitement of a live television show. It was dark and there were show staff all over the place, but the stage was awash with light as the one-man band performed. The whole thing made for an exhilarating atmosphere and, as the audience cheered and clapped along, Abby felt her heartbeat go up a few notches.

"Quickly," said Mikey, leading them along the side of the audience. A few seconds later and they were right at the side of the stage, in the wings, as it was called. From this position Abby could see Mac and look out on about half of the audience.

"OK," said Mikey. "We've got a few minutes – mind if we get some behind-the-scenes shots?"

"Of course not," said Gus generously.

Mikey made a call on his walkie-talkie and a few moments later the producer and camera operator who had filmed Ali earlier arrived and started interviewing Gus.

As she watched her father chatting away, teasing the producer and making the camera operator laugh, Abby felt a pang of something – sadness, perhaps, or maybe sympathy. Gus was a born entertainer and it must have been hard not doing what he loved these past four years.

The next moment, though, those sympathetic feelings swiftly evaporated.

"Abby!" Gus shouted, dragging Abby in front of the camera. "Tell everyone how proud you are of me."

"Um, yeah," mumbled Abby, turning beetroot. "Really proud, just, um, really proud."

"Terrific," said the producer. "See you later, good luck."

Abby was about to tell Gus never to do that to her again, but decided against it. It wasn't the right time to pick an argument; he was going onstage soon. Instead, she found herself wanting to say something genuinely sincere to him, but the right words wouldn't come, so she just straightened his tie a little.

"Everything OK?" someone said chirpily in a Scottish accent.

It was Josie, the senior producer and their contact on the inside. Abby was instantly reminded of the conversation she'd overheard about Josie having given all those instructions. She eyed her suspiciously.

"Yes, of course," said Gus.

"Great," said Josie. She leaned in closer and lowered her voice. "Just to say, I'll be in the gallery when you're on. If you spot anything, anything at all, let me know."

"Gotcha," said Gus, giving her a massive double thumbs up, which Abby thought was overdoing it, a lot.

"But we need a code word," Josie went on. "How about *tomatoes*. Drop that into your routine and I'll know."

"Tomatoes. Absolutely," said Gus,

Josie gave him a wink and then left.

Gus shook his head. "She's a bit odd," he said.

"You always said there were lots of strange people in television," said Abby. "I'm going to see if I can spot Harry."

As the one-man band trudged off the other side of the stage – he hadn't got through – Abby walked as far as she could without being seen and looked out over the audience. She couldn't find Harry amongst the bubbling lava lake of faces – but if she had, she would have seen him sitting very upright with a tense look on his face.

*

"Time now to introduce an old friend," said Mac. "You know we love giving people a second chance on *BBNS*. Four years ago we met magician Gregor the Great. He was good, but not quite good enough. Well, now he's back and he's no longer Gregor the Great. He's Gregor the Gobsmacking!"

Harry perched on the edge of his seat. He remembered what Gregor had said earlier: *They'd better not reject me again. . . There will be trouble if they do . . . big trouble.*

"Trevor?" whispered Harry into his earpiece. "Stand by."

"Stand by what?" said Trevor.

Harry groaned. "Just – pay attention," he hissed.

Gregor's intro film finished and he walked out to excited applause. He seemed relaxed enough, thought Harry, but his moustache was twitching quite a lot.

"Hello," said Diamond. "Good to see you again, Gregor. What have you been doing these last four years?"

"I've been working on my act," said Gregor. "And this time, I'm going to smash it!"

"Well," said Clive. "I hope that my gob really is well

and truly smacked tonight. Good luck."

Gregor bowed majestically. Then he pulled a newspaper out from inside his jacket.

"This is yesterday's paper," he said. "I've read it cover to cover, so I don't need it any more."

On the word *more* he ripped the paper in half, then ripped it again and again until he was left with a pile of shredded newspaper in his hands.

"Oh no!" he said. "I've just remembered, I didn't read the sports section."

He rubbed his palms together, then opened his hands and, magically, the paper was back in one piece.

The audience applauded, but Harry thought that it was polite rather than rapturous applause. They'd seen better tricks.

Gregor's act continued in similar fashion. It wasn't bad, but it wasn't that good either. Harry found himself wondering what the judges would do and, crucially, what would happen if they didn't put Gregor through to the next round.

"I'm undecided," said Eve. "But I believe in giving people second chances, so I'm going to say yes."

"Thank you, Eve," said Gregor. "Thank you so much."

Wally was next.

"Listen, Gregor," he said. "I've worked with a few magicians in my time, and my honest opinion is, you're still not quite there yet. Sorry, but it's a no from me."

Harry watched Gregor carefully. He managed a slightly sour smile, then turned to face Clive.

"Gregor, you're good," said Clive. "But you didn't smack my gob. However . . . I'm with Eve. I think you deserve a second chance. I'm giving you a yes."

Gregor breathed out and gave Clive a thumbs up.

"So, that's two yesses and one no," said Mac. "Diamond, it's all down to you."

"Oh no!" wailed Diamond. "I hate this."

Harry could see that Gregor was sweating. This was like being at the Colosseum, he thought. Thumbs up or thumbs down, what was it to be?

"We need an answer, Diamond," said Mac.

"OK," said Diamond. "Gregor, I'm a massive fan. I think you're great, but I still don't think you're ready. Sorry. It's a no."

The audience gasped, some of them booed, and one accidentally passed wind.

"Such a shame your journey has to end here, Gregor," said Mac. "But have you enjoyed your time on the show?"

As Harry watched, a change came over Gregor. He no longer looked anxious; instead, he looked menacing.

"You," he said, stepping forward and pointing a finger at the judges, "have made a mistake. A big, big mistake."

The audience didn't like that, and many of them started booing.

Gregor ignored them and stared with piercing eyes at the judges. Then he turned on his heels and marched offstage.

Harry didn't know what to make of it. Nothing terrible had happened, but Gregor seemed to be sending out a warning.

At the side of the stage, Abby watched as Gregor swept past, muttering to himself.

"Stand by, Gus," said Mikey.

Gus nodded.

"You OK, Dad?" said Abby.

"Of course, darling," he said. "I have done this sort of thing before, you know."

Yes, thought Abby. Only not for four years, and not on live television.

What could possibly go wrong?

CHAPTER 13

The Comeback Kids

"Well, you know what they say. Absence makes the comedian grow funnier!" Mac guffawed loudly. "And I am thrilled this guy is back. Here's hoping we see a lot . . . *more* . . . of him. It's Gus Moore!"

Gus's film started. It was basically a potted history of his previous career and a small mention of the incident with Mum, followed by Gus talking about how he felt the time was right for a comeback. Then, after a gentle shove from Mikey, he walked out onstage.

Abby felt a surge of excitement and panic, along with a smidgen of pride. She was sure that Harry was feeling the same.

"Thanks, Mac," said Gus, sounding relaxed and confident. "They don't make 'em much better than Mac Tatum – or MT, as I used to call him, because there's nothing going on up top, completely empty."

That got a good laugh from the audience and a showbiz smile from Mac.

"So, good evening, everyone," continued Gus. "I've had an interesting time lately. I fell off my chair playing that word game Scrabble the other day. An ambulance came and they said I was doing fine, but could do with a couple more vowels, so they took me to A and E."

That got another decent laugh, and as Gus continued, the audience warmed to him more and more. By the end, they were roaring with laughter.

The judges then went into their deliberations.

"Gus," said Wally. "I have to admit, I was worried when I heard you had entered the competition – you've had a long time out of the game. But you've come back better than ever! I loved it. You've got your first yes."

"Thank you, Wally," said Gus. "And if ever I need a new agent, I'll give you a call . . . I hear you know some good ones."

Wally laughed a bit too much at Gus's joke, but it was a good start.

"Darling, stand-up terrifies me," said Eve. "Give me a period drama any day. But you were marvellous! Soooo funny. It's a yes from me."

"Thank you, your ladyship," said Gus, bowing extravagantly.

The spotlight now moved to Clive. To Abby's surprise, he was frowning.

"Maybe as a stand-up comedian myself, my standards are too high. But to be honest, I was expecting better."

"Noooo, boooooo!" shouted a few members of the audience.

"I'm sorry, but I have to be objective," said Clive. "I can't let our friendship sway my decision, that would be unfair to the other acts, so, I'm saying no."

This time the whole place booed and jeered at Clive, but Gus just smiled and winked knowingly at him, though Clive had no idea what he was meant to know.

It was all down to Diamond now. She stood up and eyeballed Clive, screwing up her face so much her eyes disappeared and all you could see were her long lashes.

"I don't know what you were listening to, Clive," she said. "But *I* thought it was brilliant. It's a massive yes from me."

As the audience roared their approval, Abby

relaxed. Gus was through. They could continue their undercover mission.

"Congratulations, Gus, we'll see you in the semifinal!" said Mac.

Gus waved to the audience and casually walked offstage.

"Right," continued Mac. "Our next act is eggstraordinary. It's Brenda and her musical chickens!"

In the audience, Harry decided it was time to slip out and find Abby in the waiting area.

He arrived as Gus was in the middle of another behind-the-scenes interview.

"Of course I didn't take it personally. Clive's such a kidder," he was saying. "But he's a great guy really, we're big buds."

"Hey," said Harry, tapping Abby on the arm.

"Thank goodness you're here," she said. "We have got a LOT to talk about."

"We certainly have," said a voice behind them. The twins turned to see Rosy.

"Oh, hello, Rosy," said Harry. "I thought you were

in your uncle's dressing room?"

"I was," she said. "But my hand started hurting from all the notes I was taking for my file, so I decided to have a break. The show's nearly finished anyway. I left Teddy there though; he wanted to watch the end. So are you two finally going to tell me what's going on?"

"Yes," said Abby, drawing them both into the corner. "We'll tell you."

Harry looked a little startled, but he trusted that Abby knew what she was doing.

"We *are* here to support our dad," continued Abby. "But we decided that we would also do some investigating of our own."

"Because of the curse?" said Rosy, her face lighting up with excitement.

"Yes, but we don't think there *is* a curse," said Abby.

Rosy's eyes grew bigger.

"You know all those things that happened tonight? The whoopee cushions, sprinklers, the trapdoor and the lights going off?"

"And don't forget about that spanner that almost hit me," said Rosy.

"Yes, that as well," Abby said, lowering her voice to a conspiratorial whisper. "We think someone did all those things on purpose."

"Really?" said Rosy. "But what about the talking dog? He was the one who first spoke about the curse."

"More than likely that was set up by the same person," said Abby.

Rosy was thoughtful for a moment. "But all those things could ruin the show," she said, frowning. "Why would someone want to do that?"

"That is exactly what we want to find out," said Abby. "Will you help us?"

Before Rosy could answer, there was a commotion – Mac Tatum was approaching, flanked by Tanya and a small army of people: make-up artists, stylists and someone whose only job seemed to be to hold his coffee. The show was now over and, without being asked, he barged straight into the filming of Gus's backstage interview.

"Gus! Buddy!" Mac called. "You did a great job out there."

"Well, you know, you never lose it," said Gus.

"Especially if you never had it," said Mac, and the two of them hooted like hyperactive owls.

They continued larking about for a little while longer, but the moment the filming was over, Mac turned to Tanya. "Get the kids," he barked.

She nodded, turned to a young, scared-looking girl, and snapped, "You heard him. Get the kids."

Abby rolled her eyes. "We're standing right here," she said.

"Ah, there you are," said Mac. "Oh, hello Rosy. Now, Henry, Abby, I've had a brilliant idea, you're going to love it. The next show is the semi-final. If your father gets through to the final, and by *if* I mean *when*, how about you two run out onstage and gave him a huge hug?"

All the other people in Mac's mini-army clapped as if it was indeed a brilliant idea.

"Oh, that's wonderful!" said Tanya.

Harry and Abby didn't think it was a brilliant idea. In fact, they wanted to say, *Please please please don't make us do it*, but before they could say anything, Gus shrieked, "That is genius! Of course they'll do it."

"Great," said Mac, ignoring the fact that Harry and

Abby hadn't said a word. "Tanya, sort it, will you?"

"Of course," said Tanya. She turned to the girl and snapped, "Sort it."

"Wow, you're going to be on television," said Rosy to the twins. "I'm so jealous."

"Yes," said Abby, very able to contain her excitement.

"And through to the semi-final is . . . Gus Moore!" said Rosy in a cheesy, deep voice.

"Was that meant to be your uncle?" asked Harry.

"Yes, it was," said Rosy. "It's good for me to practise being a presenter."

Harry and Abby both smiled weakly. They were already thinking of ways to ensure their television debut didn't happen when, at that moment, the show's opening music started playing over the speakers.

"That's odd," said Mac, frowning.

Harry and Abby looked at each other nervously. The next second they all jumped out of their skins, as the volume went up to ear-splitting.

"What's going on?" shouted Mac to the two security guards.

"We think someone's got into the gallery and is

messing with the controls," the woman shouted back. "We're on our way."

"It's the curse," wailed Lincoln. Inevitably this set everyone off again.

"We need to get there and check this out," said Harry.

Abby and Rosy thought for a moment.

"I've got an idea," said Abby.

"Is it brilliant?" said Harry.

"Let's hope so," replied Abby.

CHAPTER 14

Ghosts in the Gallery?

"Rosy," said Abby. "Are you up for creating a diversion?"

"Maybe," said Rosy cautiously. "What would I have to do?"

"Well, could you pretend that the snake has escaped again and start screaming?"

A slightly wicked grin came over Rosy's face. "Oh yes, I can do that. It would be like acting, which I might do to become a star."

"OK," said Abby, grinning back. "I'm going to count to three. Here goes. One. Two. Three."

On the count of three, Rosy let rip with an

eardrum-busting scream, followed by terrified shouts of, "Snake! Snake!"

Along with the blaring music, the atmosphere quickly became one of panic and confusion.

"Wow, I almost believe there is a snake," said Harry admiringly.

"Great job, Rosy, keep it up," shouted Abby. "Come on, Harry, we haven't got long."

In all the chaos, Abby and Harry were able to weave through the melee and slip unnoticed to the gallery. The door was slightly open when they got there and, peering round it, they could see a group of people deep in conversation. The music had stopped. Clearly someone had hit the off button.

"What's that smell?" Harry whispered, sniffing. "It reminds me of something."

"Shhh," Abbie hissed. "Listen."

"I don't understand it," one of the security guards was saying to Josie. "The door was locked when we got here. When we opened it, there was no one inside."

"Could it have been a malfunction?" said Josie.

"It's possible," said another man doubtfully. "But very unlikely."

Josie sighed in frustration. "Well, we need some answers, otherwise we might have to delay or even cancel the final," she said. "This shouldn't be happening, the secret service are meant to be sorting this all out and . . . hey, what are you doing there?"

Everyone turned to look at Harry and Abby, hovering just by the open door.

"We . . . we were scared," said Harry. "There was a lot of noise and there was a snake on the loose and we were looking for somewhere to hide and we saw this door was open and. . ."

It seemed Rosy wasn't the only one who was a good actor.

"Don't worry," said Josie. "It's all sorted now, so if you could make your way back to the waiting area, please."

"No problem," said Harry as they retreated.

"That's interesting," whispered Abby. "If the door was locked, then who messed with the controls?"

"It must be the curse," said Harry.

Abby rolled her eyes at him, then clutched his arm. "Look!"

It was Tom, the handyman who had dropped the spanner and given Erran a pass. He was kneeling down, working on a plug socket.

As they walked past, Abby craned her neck to get a better look. It *seemed* as though he was replacing a couple of screws, but he *was* very close to the gallery. Was that just a coincidence – or had he been the one messing with the sound controls?

Another question, thought Abby. They'd have to come up with some answers soon, or who knew what might happen.

"What is it? What is it?" said Harry, sniffing the air.

"Stop it," said Abby. "You're being weird."

"It's that smell, I know it from somewhere," Harry said. "Is it food, a person, an animal. . ." He continued ruminating as they headed back to the waiting area, where everything was calm and quiet now.

"Where did you two get to?" asked Gus.

"We thought we saw the snake over there, so we chased after it," said Abby.

"Well, you were wasting your time," said Gus. "It was a false alarm. The snake was in the basket all the time."

"I'm sorry," said Rosy. "I thought I saw it and I just got scared." She hung her head, but gave Harry and Abby the faintest wink.

"Don't worry, Rosy, these things happen," said Mac. "Right, I'm exhausted. It's always the same after a big show, adrenalin one minute, then the crash. Come on, Rosy, let's go."

"The curse has struck again! The curse has struck again!"

"Oh, what is it now?!" huffed Mac, exasperated.

They all turned to see the judge, Eve, stagger in. She looked dishevelled and shocked.

"It was on my mirror when I got back to my dressing room. In blood! The words *Beware the Curse*."

As the room erupted in shock and speculation again, Tanya rushed over and, with a comforting arm around Eve's shoulder, led her out, no doubt reassuring her as they went.

A series of knowing looks passed between Harry,

Abby and Rosy. They knew this was something else to add to their investigations.

"Right, Rosy," said Mac. "Let's see if we can make it out of the door without anything else happening. Come on."

Rosy quickly turned to Harry. "Give me your hand," she said.

Harry thought it was a bit formal to shake hands, but held his out anyway.

"Here's my phone number," said Rosy, taking out a pen and writing on Harry's hand. "In case you need any more help in the week."

"Sure," said Abby. "You've been brilliant; you are totally one of the team now."

Rosy beamed. Her smile couldn't have been any bigger if she'd eaten the biggest banana in the world, sideways.

"See you at the semi-final," said Harry. "And bring your A game. If it's half as eventful as this show, we're going to be in for quite a ride."

CHAPTER 15

Parklife

"The spirits are angry," Debbie Acorn intoned calmly but menacingly. "Very, very angry."

She was sitting on a large deep-red cushion in a dark room surrounded by candles. Her face, heavily made up with black lipstick and dark eye shadow, seemed to pop in and out of view as the flickering lights danced all around.

She bowed her head and smoothed the silky fabric of her flowing white gown. Then she looked up, directly into the camera. Her green eyes were fierce.

"If you thought last night was bad, you're in for a nasty surprise," she said. "The sprinklers, the trapdoor, the lights. That was just the spirits having fun. Wait till you see what they can really do."

She stopped to let her words sink in.

"I have been contacted by an ancient spirit called Phompha. She has chosen my body as the vessel to channel her message. Come to me, Phompha."

Debbie's breathing became louder and faster until suddenly she fell backwards, her head dangling off the back of the cushion.

Slowly, she sat back up.

"I am Phompha," she announced in a completely different voice. Now it was much deeper, with a slightly Eastern European accent. "The show is desecrating my people's ancient burial lands. The new building sits atop the remains of our great and wise leaders. You were warned once, but you fools would not listen. I tell you this now. Cancel the final or next time it will be worse. A million times worse."

At that point the candles all went out and the room was plunged into darkness.

"Well," said Harry. "Phompha seems like a cheery sort."

Harry and Abby were sitting on the park bench, watching Debbie's latest show on a phone. They were waiting for Trevor. He was late again, but it was a warm day so they didn't mind too much.

"Look how many hits she's getting for these videos," said Harry thoughtfully. "She's more popular than ever." He looked at Abby. "Do you think Debbie could have masterminded everything that has happened?"

"She'd need an accomplice on the inside, then. She couldn't have written on Eve's mirror and done all those other things any other way. Seems like a lot of effort just for publicity, though," said Abby.

"Yes," said Harry. "Unless she has some other reason to ruin the show."

The two of them sat in contemplative silence for a few moments until a man wearing sunglasses and holding a newspaper sat down next to them.

"The weather in Minks is hot this year," he said.

"The people there must be very sweaty," said Harry. "And it's *Minsk*."

"That's what I said!" The man took off his glasses. "It's me, Trevor."

"We'd never have guessed," said Abby.

"I know, great disguise, eh?" said Trevor, pulling out a notebook. "Now then, I have a *lot* of notes after that show."

"Oh yes," said Abby, sitting up straighter. "It certainly was interesting, wasn't it?"

"Definitely. First off, your father was a-mazing. He's going to be huge again, I just know it. But I think he's a little rusty. His timing was a bit off and he could cut that second joke. I loved his gag about Mac, though. Genius."

"Right," said Harry. "So do you have any notes that *aren't* about our dad?"

"Yes, of course," said Trevor. "Just one more thing. Do you think you could get him to record a message

for me? Only short. Ten, maybe twenty seconds. What do you think?"

"Yes, fine, we'll ask him," said Abby. "But did you not notice anything else? Anything suspicious that might help with the *actual investigation*?"

Trevor put down his notebook. "Actually, I did," he said. "You know you said the lights going out during Blade's performance might not have been planned, Abby? I'm starting to suspect you might be right. And that's not all. I don't think the whoopee cushions, the trapdoor and the sprinklers were accidents either. Someone did all that!"

"No!" said Harry and Abby in mock surprise.

"Yes! In each case, a crew member says they were contacted by the senior producer, Josie. The person who opened the trapdoor, for instance. She swears Josie told her to do it over her walkie-talkie. But *Josie* says she did nothing of the sort. It can't have been Josie, of course, because she's our insider, but it is weird, eh?"

The twins nodded. It fitted with what Abby had overheard in the technical area, but it certainly *was* very strange.

"My bosses aren't happy," said Trevor glumly. "They're thinking of advising the royal family not to send anyone to attend the final. And the show's producers aren't happy either, because we promised them we'd get to the bottom of it. I'm getting it in both ears, I can tell you, so I hope you've got some good information."

"We have," said Harry.

"But you can't have it," said Abby. "Not yet."

"What?" shouted Trevor. "Why not?"

"As you mentioned, Dad could become a big star again after this," Abby said. "And if we help you get to the bottom of everything, you'll probably get a promotion. But what about us?"

"What do you mean?" said Trevor.

"What do *we* get out of this?" said Harry.

"I could get you some chocolate," said Trevor. "What are your favourites? Twix, Mars, Bounty. . ."

"I'm afraid that won't quite cut it," said Abby. "We were thinking that maybe you could have a word with someone about our mum."

"About getting her released from prison," said Harry.

"Oh," said Trevor uncertainly. "I don't know about that."

"Why not?" said Abby. "We know you're a VERY important agent, so you must have contacts."

"Well, yes, of course," said Trevor. "I am, and I do."

"And we have a lot of interesting information. It would be a shame not to tell you it," added Harry.

"Plus, you *have* broken the rules a teensy bit," said Abby. "If anyone were to find out you were using two children. . ."

"OK, OK," snapped Trevor. "I'll see what I can do. Now, please tell me what you've got."

"Well," said Abby. "We've got quite a few suspects. I'm sure you've already thought about Debbie Acorn."

"Oh yes, I really like *Woooooooooooo*, it's great," said Trevor.

"She's definitely using the rumours of a curse as an opportunity to get publicity for herself and her show, and it's working," said Harry. "But could she actually be behind it all herself? It seems a bit much to sabotage *BBNS* just to boost her own show."

"Yes," jumped in Abby. "And lots of people love

161

BBNS. If Debbie did ruin the show, that wouldn't make her very popular at all."

"Well, it wouldn't be her, would it? It would be the ghosts she's summoned," said Trevor. "They can be very difficult to control."

"Ha ha," laughed Abby, stopping suddenly when she realized Trevor wasn't joking. "Um. Then there's Erran the hypnotist. I saw him trick his way into the secure show staff area. I couldn't follow him, but he must have been up to something."

"He's doing well on the show, though, so we don't know why he would want to sabotage it," said Harry. "Plus he seems really nice."

"Don't be fooled," said Trevor. "The nice ones are always the most dangerous."

"There's also Tom, a handyman on the show," said Abby. "He gave Erran his pass, so maybe they're in it together. And he dropped a spanner that nearly fell on Rosy's head. She's Mac's niece. A tragic accident would *definitely* put a stop to the show."

"Then there's Gregor the magician," said Harry. "Before the show I heard him say that if he didn't get through, there would be trouble. And then we all heard what he said to the judges onstage. *You've made a big mistake.*"

"Surely if he was behind everything he wouldn't make a serious threat in front of everyone," said Abby. "It's a bit obvious."

"Hiding in plain sight," said Trevor. "Clever tactic."

"Next on our list is Ali the snake charmer," said Abby. "I overheard her on the phone saying everything was going to plan, and that she hadn't been recognized. I don't know why she'd want to scupper the show, but we already know she can do a lot of damage with her snake."

"Horrible creatures," said Trevor, shuddering. "If she works with them, she's definitely up to no good. Keep an eye on her. Is that it?"

"No. There's Tanya, the deputy senior producer," said Harry.

"Yes," said Abby. "I saw a message on her phone about losing her job and how *they* were going to regret doing that to her."

"So we checked last night," said Harry. "She was the

senior producer for the last three series, but now Josie has come in, Tanya has been demoted."

"Inside job," said Trevor. "Interesting."

"Well, talking of that," said Abby. "What *about* Josie?"

Trevor stared at her. "But – but she called us! And her uncle worked for the service. Impossible."

"Maybe," said Abby. "But we can't ignore the fact that those stagehands said it was definitely her giving them instructions. And we checked her out. She used to work for *Britain's Top Act*."

"*BBNS*'s rival show!" gasped Trevor.

"Exactly. What if she's *still* working for them and that's why she is out to destroy *BBNS*?"

"A double agent," murmured Trevor. "All right, keep her under surveillance as well. Anything else?"

"Erm, I did hear some people talking about Mac," said Abby.

"Mac?" said Trevor. "Mac Tatum?"

"Yes," said Abby. "There's a theory going round that he's behind everything because he knows he's getting fired at the end of the series."

"We talked about it," said Harry. "And he did seem to be genuinely shocked and confused by the 'accidents', but he could be a good actor, and he did recover his composure pretty quickly."

"Maybe he and Josie are in it together," mused Trevor. "Good work. Right, if that's it I've got to. . ."

"Weeeell, there is one more thing," said Harry. "This might be nothing, but do you remember Angie? The nine-year-old singer."

"Yes, of course," said Trevor. "Voice like an angel."

"Here we go, you're going to love this, Trevor," said Abby sarcastically.

Harry ignored her and continued. "As we know from her film, the family don't have much. But I sat next to her dad in the audience and he was wearing what looked like a very expensive watch."

Harry took out his phone and scrolled through a lot of very blurry pictures before he came to one which was much clearer. He showed it to Trevor.

"Probably a fake," said Trevor a little snottily. "But tell me more."

"Well, I did a bit of digging last night," said Harry.

"And it seems that before *BBNS* bought the new studio building, another company wanted it. A very big company that own loads of properties. They were going to demolish it and build flats. What if they were really angry that *BBNS* got the building? They found out about Angie being on the show and they're paying her family loads of money to scupper it!"

"I do love it. You were right, Abby," said Trevor.

"He hasn't finished yet," said Abby.

"With the money they paid them, Angie's dad bought a super-watch. My friend Naresh told me about them, he says he knows for certain they exist. They emit sonic sound waves that can make people do all sorts of things. It could explain a lot."

"It's a ridiculous theory," said Abby at the same time that Trevor said, "Amazing work, send me the photo, Harry!"

"So what are the next steps?" said Abby, shaking her head.

"You've done well," said Trevor. "Lots of leads, we'll run some checks and let you know if anything comes up. In the meantime, pursue all of them."

It was the most professional and spy-like he'd ever sounded. Sadly, the next moment, he blew it.

"But most importantly ... please, please, please don't forget to ask your dad to film that message for me. Just a quick hello and a gag or two. You won't forget, will you?"

"We won't," said Abby. "Bye, Trevor."

The twins got up and walked off. It was a beautiful, sunny day, the birds were singing, children were playing. But something felt wrong.

"Do you get the feeling. . ." Abby said.

"That we're being followed? Yeah," said Harry.

Abby looked at Harry. "On three," she whispered. "One, two, three!"

They both swung round.

Mum!

"Oh no," said Harry. "What are you doing here?"

"That's not a very nice way to greet your mother," Samantha said, sounding hurt. "I wanted to see you two."

"We want to see you, Mum," said Abby. "But you know you're not meant to escape. Wouldn't it be better if we came during prison visiting hours?"

"Where's the fun in that?" said Mum. "Anyway, I'm not staying long, they won't even know I'm gone. I have something important to tell you."

"Right," said the twins. Mum's important messages were legendary in the Moore family, mainly for not being very important at all.

"It's Aunt Valerie's dog's fifth birthday next week," she said. "Please don't forget to send a card, you know how she gets."

"We won't," said Abby. "And Mum ... wouldn't it be nice if you were home for good and we could be a normal family again? You do want that, don't you?"

"Of course," said Mum. "Oh look, a squirrel."

"Where?" said Abby, as both she and Harry glanced at the trees. "Mum? Mum?"

Samantha had disappeared. She really was extremely good at escaping.

The twins arrived home to a pile of dirty dishes and a very full laundry basket.

"I bet real undercover agents don't have to do this," said Harry, making a start on the dishes.

"That's because they don't have a father like ours," said Abby, picking up a small mountain of smelly clothes.

"Ah, good, you're back," said Gus. "I was just about to do that myself."

"Of course you were, Dad," said Harry.

"Now then," said Gus. "I've been thinking about what Mac said, you know, about you coming onstage when I get through to the final."

"*If* you get through to the final, Dad," corrected Harry.

"Yes, yes," said Gus. "The thing is, I'm not sure about it."

"Oh good, neither are we," said Abby, relieved.

"Yeah, it's a bit tame, isn't it?" said Gus. "I'm going to come up with something much more exciting, a proper comedy moment. Watch this space."

Gus wandered out as casually as he'd wandered in. He hadn't offered to help with the chores and he'd made the prospect of them going onstage a trillion times worse.

"Right, that's it," said Abby. "I don't care about the show or the royal family or anything any more. I'm contacting the secret service and telling them to make sure he doesn't get through to the final."

"Hmm," said Harry. "Our only contact is Trevor, and something tells me he might not be so keen on that."

"Aaaaaarrrggggh," screamed Abby, burying her face in the dirty washing. It turned out to be underwear, which didn't help the situation much.

"Oh, one more thing," said Gus, wandering back in. "I found this in my pocket. Looks like one of those earpod things. Does it belong to either of you?"

He put the object on the table and strolled back out. Harry and Abby stared at it. They were no experts, but they knew it wasn't an earpod. They were pretty certain it was a bugging device.

Panic-stricken, they looked at each other with the same question in their heads.

Was someone on to them?

CHAPTER 16
To Plan or Not to Plan

The warnings were clear, but you did not listen.

Do not test my patience.

The show is doomed.

If you continue to the final I will have my revenge and wreak havoc in front of the whole country.

Cancel it now, or else!

"Well?" said Trevor. "What do you think?"

"I think . . . it sounds like a threatening note," said Abby, stating the obvious.

"Fascinating!" said Trevor, who had read the note to the twins over the phone. "Mac got one. So did the judges and Josie. And the strangest thing is, they were sent from Romania, but that's all top-secret classified information, so not a word to anyone. Apart from me, of course."

Harry and Abby liked the idea of being party to top-secret info, but the truth was that aside from the letters, the week running up to the semi-final had been pretty uneventful. There was a lot of talk of ghosts and curses online, and in the press, and of course, Debbie was still ranting on her show, but no more speaking animals had appeared.

Gregor the Gobsmacking had stayed quiet too. Maybe he'd cooled off, the twins thought.

Gus had spent much of the week working on his routine for the semi-final. He also appeared on breakfast television with Angie. It had gone well until the host asked Gus what he thought of Angie's performance.

"I think she's a wonderful dancer," he said.

"Erm, she's a singer," said the host.

"She sings as well?" said a surprised Gus. "Well, I never."

But apart from that, the week passed quietly for the twins – school, watching Gus practise his routine, a few messages from Rosy saying how much she was looking forward to seeing them again at the weekend and the occasional update from Trevor, who hadn't discovered anything new at all.

It felt like a million miles away from the undercover world the twins had been in, so come Saturday morning, when the papers screamed "MOST EXCITING *BBNS* SEMI-FINAL YET", they were more than ready to dive headlong back into the fray.

Gus, Abby and Harry arrived at the studio building around lunchtime. There were way more security guards than last time. Debbie and her followers were there again, but they were being kept far away from the entrance.

"Good luck," Trevor told them through their earpieces as they walked in. "We've told staff to double-check any instructions they receive over their walkie-talkies. And, um, I've banned spanners. But be careful. If Gus has been bugged, someone probably knows what you're up to."

The atmosphere in the contestants' waiting area was

much the same as it had been for the previous round. Harry, Abby and Gus walked into a cacophony of nervous anticipation and agitation. There might have been fewer acts now, but they were making up for it by being twice as loud and excited.

Harry and Abby were also nervous and excited, but for different reasons. They had a long list of potential suspects. It was time to start whittling them down – and today might be the day that whoever was intent on sabotaging the show made their next move. It was going to be tricky keeping an eye on ALL of them.

Abby, being Abby, had drawn up a roster for herself and allocated a certain amount of time to watch each suspect, with room for notes.

Harry, being Harry, had refused to be tied down to a roster. He wanted to simply go with the flow and see where things took him. "Do you really need that?" he sighed.

"Being organized is the key to success," Abby said, looking at her roster. "Ali's first on my list. You should stay here with Dad. It's pretty crowded. Whoever planted that bug on him might well try and do it again."

"Why can't *you* stay with Dad?" said Harry, a little peeved.

They were still arguing when Rosy walked in.

"Hey, Rosy, great to see you again," said Abby enthusiastically.

"Yes. How are you?" said Harry.

In terms of the argument the twins were having, asking Rosy a question was a mistake. She focused her attention squarely on Harry and said, "I'm very excited to carry on with our secret mission. I've created a new file on my phone for it. Maybe after I get fed up being a big star I might become a spy. What do you want me to do?"

"Harry will brief you, Rosy," said Abby before Harry could say anything. "I'm going to find Ali. See you later."

It wasn't difficult to find Ali. She was wearing a bright red outfit this time and her arms were covered in bangles which jangled when she moved.

She was sitting reading with one hand firmly on the basket. Clearly nothing was going to escape from it today – at least, not by accident.

She wasn't wearing her glasses, though, which Abby thought was odd given what Erran had said about her eyesight.

As Abby watched, Ali took out a mirror and, very slightly, adjusted her hairline.

It's a wig! thought Abby. Time for a chat.

"Hi," said Abby, sauntering over.

"Oh, hi," said Ali, quickly putting the mirror back in her bag and taking out her glasses. She put them on. "Just had something in my eye."

"I'm Abby, Gus Moore's daughter. He's the one who knocked over your basket. Sorry about that."

"Oh, no worries," said Ali. "Ancient history."

"How's Bertie?" said Abby.

"Very well," said Ali. "He's just eaten a juicy mouse so he's probably fast asleep now."

Just then, Ali's phone rang. "Excuse me," she said, taking the phone out of her handbag, which was on the floor next to the basket. "Hi, Mum. I can't talk now, sorry, call you later."

Ali hung up, but then dropped the phone on the floor by Abby's feet.

"Sorry," she said. "Bit nervous, you know, it's the semi-final."

"Of course," said Abby, picking up the phone. "It must be terrifying onstage. I don't know how you do it."

"It is pretty terrifying," said Ali. "You can just drop it back in my bag, thanks."

Abby put the phone in Ali's bag, but as she did so, she noticed a set of house keys. A set of keys with a tag on them that read CLIVE DEREK.

Why did Ali have keys to Clive Derek's house? This was getting more and more intriguing, but Abby didn't get a chance to investigate further, as Ali was called to rehearse.

"Hey, where's Rosy?" said Abby when she was back with Harry and Gus.

"I sent her to go and make friends with Angie;

they're about the same age. I thought it was a good idea," said Harry.

"You didn't tell her your mad theory, did you?"

"Yes, I did, as a matter of fact," said Harry. "And she didn't think it was mad at all. And we also worked out a system of undercover code words."

"Go on," said Abby.

"Schnorbitz means, *I need to talk to you now.* Bluebottle means, *You are in danger,* and Farnsworth means, *We are being watched.*"

Abby smiled. She recognized those words; they were all related to comedy from years ago. Schnorbitz was a dog belonging to comedy duo Mike and Bernie Winters. Bluebottle was a character from an early radio comedy called *The Goon Show* and Farnsworth appeared in a sketch performed by the legendary actor and comedian Peter Sellers. She and Harry had been introduced to some of Gus's heroes at an early age.

"Well done," she said. "Right, next on my roster is Tom the Handyman, then Erran. You could cover Erran if you wanted to, Harry. I think we can risk leaving Dad for a little while. "

"No thanks," said Harry. "I've got another idea. But I might not stick to it. I'm easy, you know."

"Fine," said Abby. "Well, good luck with ... whatever you decide to do."

She wandered off, leaving Harry thinking, *What am I going to do?*

He looked around. Gus was sitting quietly working on his lines. No one had approached him, so it seemed reasonable that he would be fine. It was also very hot in the waiting area, so Harry decided to go outside for some fresh air and a chance to clear his head. He could also check in with Trevor.

"See you later, Dad," he said. Gus, who was muttering to himself, barely looked up.

Once outside, Harry found a quiet road and said into his mike, "Agent 4905-3, it's Harry, over."

"Receiving you loud and clear, Harry, over," said Trevor.

"Did you find out about the watch, over?" said Harry.

"Negative," said Trevor. "Over."

"Oh," said Harry. "Why not?"

"Because I accidentally deleted the photo," said

Trevor. "Could you resend? Over."

Harry sighed and said he would.

"Good work," said Trevor. "And – you haven't forgotten, have you? About the message from your dad."

"Oh. No, I haven't. Over and out," said Harry.

He resent the photo, wishing that Trevor might be reassigned and they could work with someone a little more competent, when a huge car with blacked-out windows turned into the road.

Instinctively, Harry dropped behind a tree and watched as the car parked and a chauffeur in a peaked cap got out. He walked round to the kerbside passenger door and opened it. A woman stepped out wearing what looked like a designer coat, and sunglasses. As Harry watched, she took the coat off, revealing faded old jeans, a crumpled, unironed blouse and scruffy trainers.

Harry almost yelped in surprise. It was Angie's mother.

This was very interesting and very odd. The show had sent a taxi to come and collect Harry, Abby and Gus. But this was a very fancy car.

As far as Harry was concerned, this was red-hot evidence to support his theory. Clearly the property company must have already paid Angie's family a lot of money for disrupting the show and they had already bought themselves a posh car and a chauffeur!

Harry edged further behind the tree and waited as the car drove off and Angie's mother walked towards the studio building. Then he hurried back himself, excited to prove to Abby that his theory wasn't ridiculous.

Inside the contestants' area, he spotted Rosy chatting to Angie, whose mum was now sitting nearby. He couldn't see Abby, but Gus was talking to Nick, the comedian, who this time was wearing a red jacket with yellow squares on it. He had also dyed his hair green, a combination which made Harry feel a little sick.

"Your advice last time was really helpful, Mr Moore," he was saying as he scratched his ear. "It raised my performance up a level. I can't thank you enough."

"Hi, I'm Harry, Gus's son," said Harry, interrupting.

"Hi, Harry," said Nick. "Sorry, I've probably taken your seat, haven't I?"

"Oh, that's OK," said Harry. "I can stand here."

"No, really," said Nick. "I'm off to the canteen to get a drink, I'm parched."

"He'll go far," said Gus, as Harry slumped into the chair. "Though maybe not in comedy."

Harry managed a vague smile at his dad's quip. Then he froze. There was Erran the hypnotist – AND he was talking to Tom the handyman!

Harry craned his neck to get a better look, and sure enough, lurking nearby was Abby. The twins gave each other a discreet nod.

As Harry watched, Tom removed his access-all-areas pass, which was on a lanyard around his neck, then the two of them walked off in different directions, with Erran slipping the lanyard around *his* neck as he headed away.

Abby jerked her head at Harry, then set off after Tom. Harry nodded and set off after Erran.

To his dismay, Erran was heading to the secure staff area. Harry's mind fizzed. There were security guards in place. How could he get past? Rosy!

He slalomed quickly through the throng. She was still deep in conversation with Angie.

"Sorry, excuse me," he said, practically sticking his head between the two of them. "I really need to borrow Rosy."

He grabbed Rosy's hand and led her away.

"You should have said Schnorbitz," said Rosy.

"Argh, yes, sorry, forgot," panted Harry. "I need you to help me get past security and into the staff area. I've got a lead on a suspect. I thought you could. . ."

"Leave it to me," said Rosy.

Moments later they approached the security guards. "Hello," said Rosy with imploring eyes. "I'd like to see Mac Tatum, please."

The guards smiled in a way that said, *Ahh, here's a harmless little fly that we need to swat away.*

"Afraid not, darling," said the woman. "But Mac sometimes does autographs after the show. Why don't you try again then? Run along, now."

"He'll be in his dressing room," said Rosy. "I know the way. I'm his niece."

The guards' expressions changed as if they were the ones who'd just been swatted. "One moment, please," said the man. He walked a short distance away and spoke into his walkie-talkie. A few moments later he returned.

"I'll take you now," he said.

"Can my friend come too?" Rosy said, ever so sweetly. "Uncle Mac said it was OK."

"Of course," said the guard.

The three of them walked down the corridor.

"It's OK, I know the way," said Rosy.

"But I should really. . ."

"It's fine, I know how busy you are," said Rosy firmly. "I'll definitely tell Uncle Mac how helpful you've been, though. Thanks."

And with that, Rosy swept Harry further down the corridor, leaving the security guard looking after them.

"Rosy, you were brilliant," said Harry. "I'm so pleased you're helping us."

Rosy beamed. "Why are we here?" she asked.

"I'm following Erran the hypnotist. You see, he got the handyman Tom to give him. . ."

Harry skidded to a halt and pulled Rosy into a doorway as Erran suddenly emerged from a room further down the corridor. He was clutching a plastic bag. He looked furtively around. Fortunately, he hadn't spotted Harry and Rosy. They followed some distance behind as he made his way along the corridor before turning left at the end.

Harry and Rosy scurried quickly after him.

"I'm afraid this is where I have to go it alone," whispered Harry, looking around the corner Erran had turned down.

"Why?" said Rosy.

"He's just gone into the men's toilet. I'll meet you later back in the contestants' area."

"OK," whispered Rosy.

Harry quietly slipped into the loo. He didn't know what he was going to do, which was unusual, because generally when you go into a toilet you know exactly what you're going to do.

The cubicle door at the end was shut, but all the others were empty. Erran was the only person who could possibly be inside.

Harry's heart was thumping away as if someone was playing a big bass drum inside his chest. They were both somewhere they weren't meant to be, he thought, and Erran had gone to a lot of trouble to secretly get there. Harry didn't know what Erran was up to, but he was pretty certain he wouldn't want anyone to know he was there. Plus, Erran was in league with Tom, someone who may have deliberately dropped a spanner which nearly hit a young girl. That meant Erran could well be dangerous. If he came out and saw Harry. . .

DIDDLE EE DEE DEE DEE DEE DIDDLE EE DEE DEE DEE DEE

It was Harry's phone. He'd forgotten to switch it to silent. He ran over to a sink and, with his back to the cubicles, started stabbing buttons to try and turn it off.

DIDDLE EE DEE DEE DEE DEE

That big bass drum had been replaced by a whole marching band now, and as Harry finally managed to turn his phone off, he heard someone come out of the end cubicle and walk out of the toilet.

It had to have been Erran, but had he seen Harry? Harry had no way of knowing. He leant back against the wall, taking deep breaths to calm down.

It took him a few moments, but, when he felt ready, he left the toilet and looked up and down the corridor.

There was no sign of Erran. He'd gone.

Harry had lost him.

CHAPTER 17

Big Ideas, Big Problems, Big Bother

"I lost him," Harry said miserably.

He was back in the contestants' area, where Rosy and Abby were waiting for him. Gus was off rehearsing.

"Well, to be precise, I had to let him go because my phone went off," continued Harry. "It was Trev. . ."

Harry stopped. He realized they hadn't told Rosy the whole truth and mentioning Trevor might be problematic.

". . . or . . . Trevor, my friend from school."

"Bad luck," said Abby, jumping in quickly to help

him out. "Tom just went back to work, so I didn't find anything out from him."

"Well, I'm not sure I did that well either," said Rosy. "Angie talked about what had happened to her since the first show, mainly being on television with your dad and getting lots of messages of support. She also said Josie had sent her a bunch of flowers after the show. She said her family had never seen such beautiful flowers, but that was it."

"Hmm," said Abby.

"And I asked her about the accidents and if she thought it really was the curse."

"What did she say?" said Abby.

"She just said she didn't know," said Rosy.

"Well, I saw her mum arrive in a really fancy chauffeur-driven car," said Harry confidently. "So something's going on."

"Yes, and that something could be that the show organized it as a treat for her," said Abby.

"I suppose that's possible, yes," said Harry, somewhat deflated.

"I'd say it was probable. Right, I think we need to

focus our attention elsewhere. The next person on my list is Tanya. Did you see her, Harry?"

"No, I didn't," said Harry, a little sullenly. "Maybe she quit."

"I doubt it," said Abby. "The ratings for the first show were huge. This curse business has got everyone talking. The whole country will be watching the semi-final to see what happens next."

"If only we had more time," said Harry. "The final is next weekend. A member of the royal family is meant to be coming. If we don't figure this out soon, I dread to think what might happen."

The serious mood was broken, or rather, smashed to smithereens, when Gus returned from his rehearsal in a very excitable state.

"I've got it, you're going to love this!" he boomed. "When I get through to the final, you two come rushing out *as if* you are going to hug me, I bend down – and then you run past me and hug Mac. What do you think?"

"I ... I mean we ... I mean, you, if you think it might work, I suppose. . ." said Abby.

"I knew you'd love it," said Gus, somehow interpreting what Abby had said as enthusiasm.

"Actually, Dad," said Harry, remembering Trevor's request, "a friend of mine is a big fan and would love a message from you."

"Of course," said Gus. "Anything for my fans. But the lighting here is wrong. Let's go over to that corner. No, actually, let's try over there with the natural light."

Harry stifled a groan. He had a feeling this was going to take a lot longer than he would have liked.

"Why don't we look for Tanya now?" Rosy said to Abby. "I think Harry might be busy for a while. . ."

"Good idea," said Abby. "I think it's definitely best to leave them to it."

Twenty minutes later, Harry was filming Gus in their fifth location. They'd already tried every corner of the waiting area, the canteen – "Too busy and the smell of coffee is overpowering," Gus had said – *and* the foyer.

Now they were back where they had started.

"I think that one's perfect, Dad," Harry said desperately. "Take a look."

"No, my hair isn't quite right," said Gus, looking critically at the video. "Let's go again."

"Aaaaaaaaaaaaaaarrrrggggggghhhhhh! You are the most infuriating, annoying, silly, stupid bumhead in the world!" is what Harry wanted to say. Instead, he bit his lip and said, "Fine, whatever you want, Dad."

As he waited for Gus to rearrange the single hair that had been out of place, he spotted Abby and Rosy returning. He waved miserably at them.

It only took three more attempts, but finally Gus was happy. In any case, they wouldn't have been able to film it again, because just then Josie entered, and walking a little behind her was Tanya. *She definitely hasn't quit, then*, thought Harry.

The waiting area became expectantly quiet as the two of them walked to the centre.

"First of all," said Josie. "Huge congratulations to all of you for making it to the semi-final!"

A spontaneous cheer and applause erupted in the room.

"Haven't they all done well, Tanya?"

For a moment Tanya looked startled, almost as if

someone had just poured a glass of water over her. Speaking to everyone had clearly not been in the script. Josie had caught her off guard.

"Yes," she blurted out. "What a great achievement you've all . . . achieved."

Tanya's face burnt a bright red.

Did Josie put Tanya on the spot just to assert her authority? thought Abby. Or was there more to it?

"Thank you, Tanya," said Josie. "Wonderful words. Now, as I'm sure you all know, the show has been a huge hit, and that is thanks to all of you."

"And a certain curse," muttered Abby to Harry.

"But tonight is going to be bigger and better, and by the end of it, some of you will be in the final. We're starting soon, so good luck to you all!"

The room erupted again and Josie and Tanya walked off, waving and smiling. Suddenly, above all the clapping and cheering, there was a loud scream, followed by a thud. Everyone looked over to see Josie sprawled on the floor with her glasses lying a few metres away.

"I'm *so* sorry," said Tanya, bending down to help her

up. "How clumsy of me. I can barely walk in these new shoes."

"Thank you, Tanya, I can manage," said Josie, getting herself up and dusting herself down. One of the BMX bikers picked up Josie's glasses and handed them to her.

"Don't worry, I'm OK," Josie said briskly. "Just a little accident."

"Yes, just an accident," Tanya repeated. "Have a great show, everyone!"

The two of them walked out with Tanya in front and Josie, still slightly dazed, following her.

"That was weird," said Harry.

"Hmm, yes," said Abby. "Accident or not, Tanya is definitely high up on our list of suspects. We can't waste time. We really need to get to work."

"You're right," said Rosy determinedly. "I was going to watch the show in Uncle Mac's room and take more notes, but I'm staying here to help you two."

"Great," said Harry. "So, Abs, who's next on the roster?"

Abby was just about to tell Harry, and congratulate

him on coming round to her way of thinking, when a sunny voice behind them wafted through.

"Hello, how are we all doing today?"

Harry, Abby and Rosy turned to see Tanya beaming down at them. She'd come back to the waiting area and was clearly trying very hard to be pleasant. It was as if she'd had some sort of personality transplant, Harry thought. The overall effect, though, was a bit over the top.

"We're . . . good," said Harry, blinking slightly as she smiled harder.

"Wonderful!" said Tanya. "And your day is about to get even better, because the two of you are going to be spending the show in the wings by the side of the stage. You'll be right by the action. Exciting!"

"Why?" said Abby.

"Well," said Tanya, forcing her smile even wider. "Because you could be going onstage later, and we can't have you wandering off and missing that special moment, can we? So all of us are going to stay there together to watch the whole show. "

"But it wouldn't happen till the end," said Abby. "So. . ."

"We can't take any chances, can we?" said Tanya. "Oh, we're going to have such fun together!"

"Can I come too?" asked Rosy.

"Of course," said Tanya. "Now let's go, shall we?"

"But what about Dad?" said Harry. "We usually help him get ready."

"That is sooooo sweet. But don't worry. Mikey will make sure he's where he needs to be in plenty of time."

They twins gave each other a resigned look and followed Tanya as she ushered them and Rosy along.

It did seem strange for Tanya to be taking them quite so early, but was that just the show being super-prepared and making sure everything ran smoothly this time, or was there more to it? Was Tanya the person who had bugged Gus? Did she know why Harry and Abby were really there? And if so, was she doing this to get them out of the way and sabotage the show?

They had no way of knowing, but it seemed the only plan now was to do no more investigating.

And that could spell disaster.

CHAPTER 18

Gone to the Dogs

"Welcome to the semi-final of *Britain's Biggest New Star!*" proclaimed Mac. "It's the biggest night of the competition so far, we are live to the nation and tonight, we find out who is going to make it . . . to the final!!"

Right on cue, the stage lit up in an impressive display of lights and pyrotechnics, and the audience went wild.

"I can't believe you could be out there," said Rosy, pointing to where Mac was onstage. "That's so exciting. You must tell me all about it so I can write it down."

The three of them were in the wings, sitting on large black-and-silver storage crates that had presumably contained much of the show's technical equipment. Tanya was hovering nearby, talking on her phone.

"I guess," muttered Harry. He wanted to be searching for clues and interviewing suspects, not stuck there waiting for a stage-managed embrace with Mac.

A huge band opened the show, the Hallowed Halls, after which Mac introduced the judges.

"We have an incredible show for you tonight, but first it's time to introduce four people who are super canny fragile luvvies experts and ferocious. It's our judges!"

The judges came out and did their signature moves – this time Clive pretended he had a dress on and curtsied – but instead of taking their seats, they stayed where they were on the stage.

"Judges, you look sensational," simpered Mac. "But ladies and gentlemen, tonight we're not having four judges … we've having *five*! So, will you please welcome … Greta!"

A jolt of surprise zapped around the audience as Clive's dog, Greta, came bounding out from backstage and ran excitedly up to her owner.

"Welcome, Greta, great to have you with us tonight.

Now, what will you be looking for from our semi-finalists?" asked Mac.

Greta looked up at Clive with her long tongue out and her tail wagging like an out-of-control metronome.

"Oh dear," said Mac. "What's the matter? Cat got your tongue?"

The audience roared at that one, which made Greta bark.

"Ah, I see you've found your voice," said Mac. "So tell me, once upon a time, you told us the show was CURSED! Is it true?"

"Oh, that. I was just having a laugh," said Greta in a silly, high-pitched voice.

There was a stunned silence. Then the audience realized it was Clive speaking. They roared with laughter again.

Harry looked at Abby. They knew what was going on. This was the show sending out a message. *If we can laugh about this curse thing, it must be nonsense.*

"My friend Debbie Acorn told me to do it," said Greta/Clive.

"That must make you the first living creature she's

198

spoken to in a while," said Mac. "Thank you, Greta. Judges, to your seats!"

The audience applauded wildly as the judges sat down, Greta perching on Clive's lap.

"Greta didn't speak like that in the video," said Rosy. "It was a silly voice."

Harry and Abby nodded. The whole thing seemed pretty silly to them, given they should have been searching for clues.

"Right, it's almost time for our first act," said Mac. "And remember: tonight, *you* the viewers decide who goes through to the final. It's all down to your votes! The judges might as well have stayed at home, it would have saved us a fortune in hairspray. I'm kidding, we wouldn't do it without them."

"I hate this," whispered Harry. "What if something happens?"

"We'll just have to do what we can from here," whispered Abby. "If we see any of our suspects doing anything unusual, we run out there and stop them."

"Great plan," said Harry. "And if we're wrong we'll blow our cover AND look like idiots on national TV."

Abby sighed. "We don't have much choice," she said, adding much more quietly so that Rosy wouldn't hear, "Trevor would never be able to send his team in in time anyway."

There were three acts in the first part of the show: the pianist, the BMX bikers and then the father-and-son singing duo.

After a break, the second part started with Blade, the knife thrower. Tension was high as he came on, but even though he did well, his act didn't reach the dramatic heights of the previous round.

"Time now for our little heartbreaker with an incredible voice," said Mac. "This, ladies and gentlemen, is Angie."

As Angie's film started to play, she and her father appeared near to where Harry and Abby were. Harry instantly tensed up, but Abby just rolled her eyes.

"Hey, you two, looking forward to your big moment?"

It was Erran, the hypnotist. He had an assistant producer with him.

"Can't wait," said Harry, eyeing him suspiciously whilst trying not to eye him suspiciously.

"I'm running a bit late," said Erran. "I had to go to the toilet. Jane here is not happy with me."

What?! thought a startled Harry. Had Erran mentioned the toilet on purpose? Was he toying with them?

"Erran," said Jane. "Change of plan. They've told me they want you to enter from the other side. Come on."

"Seems I have to go," said Erran. "See you later."

Erran headed off with Jane, leaving Harry in quite a tailspin.

"He is definitely up to something," muttered Harry. "This is so infuriating!"

"Keep it together, soldier," said Abby. "Remember, at the first sign of any trouble, we go."

Onstage, Angie's film had nearly finished. Abby glanced over. She was still standing with her father, who was talking to her. Rosy waved, but Angie didn't notice.

"Just remember what we said about your voice," Abby heard Angie's father say to her. "Keep it, you know, how we discussed."

Angie nodded.

"I didn't know Angie's father was her vocal coach," said Abby.

"Neither did I," said Harry, trying as discreetly as he could to get a look at Angie's father's watch. Just then Angie's film finished and she stepped out onstage to thunderous applause, with her father looking on anxiously after her.

She told the judges that she'd decided to sing "I Will Always Love You".

"Sweetheart," said Diamond. "That is such a big song, and soooo difficult!"

The other judges nodded in agreement and looked suitably concerned.

"You can do it, Angie!" shouted someone from the audience.

"Let's hope so," said Diamond. "Good luck, darling."

The lights went down and a spotlight fell on Angie. She started singing. As before, Harry thought her performance was distinctly average. Once again, though, the judges could not have been more gushing in their praise. Angie went bright red and looked at her feet.

"Well, Angie," said Mac, kneeling down. "What do you make of those comments?"

"I ... I'm really pleased," said Angie. "I hope the

people at home aren't . . . ain't going to forget to vote for me. I so want to get to the final and change my family's life for ever."

"I'm sure they won't," said Mac. "They love you. Give it up one more time for Angie."

The audience applauded wildly and Angie scurried off. Rosy waved to her again as she went past and to her father who was standing a little way back in the wings.

"Look," whispered Harry, nudging Abby. She watched as the two of them walked away in complete silence.

"Isn't that weird?" said Harry. "Her dad was cheering and crying when he was in the audience. Now it's like they're barely speaking."

"Maybe his super-watch has a setting which disrupts people's moods," said Abby, smiling.

Harry ignored her.

Erran was up next.

"Thank you," he said as he came on. "So, hello, judges, how are we all today?"

The judges gave him a thumbs up and smiled.

"Good, good," Erran continued. "And have you all had something to eat before the show? Because I think one of you ate a bit too fast, isn't that right, Wally?"

No sooner had Erran said Wally's name than he hiccuped.

"Oh dear, Wally," said Erran.

Wally hiccuped again. In fact, every time Erran said Wally's name, he hiccuped. And he said it a lot. All throughout the rest of his act. He had people up onstage doing all sorts of things and suddenly he'd shout, "Wally," and Wally would hiccup.

To finish, he said "Wally" eight times in quick succession. It was hilarious.

"Well, well, well," said Mac. "What did you think, Wally?"

"Hiccup!"

Wally loved it, as did the other three judges.

"Another star turn, Erran," said Mac. "I don't think Wally" – hiccup – "will ever bolt his food again. How are you feeling after that?"

"Fantastic," said Erran. "I hope people at home liked it because I'd love to make the final. I have something very special planned."

"Did you hear that?" Harry whispered. "He's

definitely playing with us. He's telling everyone that he's going to do something in the final. He's getting really cocky."

"Or," said Abby, "he might be telling people that he has a big performance prepared if he gets through."

"Maybe," said Harry. "But why was he getting a pass from Tom, and why did he need to get into the secure show staff area?"

Abby didn't have an answer for that.

Another break followed, and at the start of the next part Mac introduced Nick, the young comedian. His short film played and he was just about to walk out onstage when Rosy suddenly exclaimed, "Look! Over there!"

Harry and Abby looked out in to the audience. Someone was out of their seat and heading down the aisle. He was wearing a hat tugged down over his face, but there was something very familiar about him. He was heading for the judges.

"Tanya," gasped Abby. "What's happening?"

Incredibly, Tanya just smiled.

The audience had noticed him now and were

clearly confused. Was this part of Nick's act, or was it something more sinister? Harry looked at Abby and nodded.

"Trevor," he whispered. "We're going in. There's an intruder in the studio. Backup needed."

Suddenly, Wally leapt to his feet. "What are you doing?" he shouted. The man was right in front of Wally now. He raised his hand up. He had something in it.

"No, don't," shouted Wally.

The next moment two plain-clothed security guards leapt out of the audience and swiftly grabbed the man, who yelped, stumbled, and tipped a carton of something all over himself. He was covered in white gloop.

"Is that . . . yoghurt?" whispered Harry.

One of the security guards yanked off the intruder's hat. It was Gregor the Gobsmacking.

"What a waste of good yoghurt," said Mac from the stage. "Nice to see you again, Gregor, we were expecting you. Great acting, by the way, Wally. Now don't worry folks, we'll make sure he does a very quick disappearing act so we can get on with the show."

The audience booed and jeered as a dripping Gregor was led away.

"They knew he was coming," said Harry.

"Yes, I'd worked that out," said Abby thoughtfully.

"That was very interesting," said Rosy. "I took lots of notes, but I don't understand something. Do you think Gregor was behind all the weird things that have been happening?"

Harry and Abby looked at each other. They very much doubted it.

CHAPTER 19

Snakes Everywhere

"Poor old Gregor. I just hope it wasn't organic yoghurt. That stuff is expensive!"

Nick got a small laugh from the audience for that line, which, unfortunately, turned out to be the high point of his performance. It went badly downhill from there and Eve summed things up afterwards when she said, "The funniest thing about your act is your jacket, and even that isn't *that* funny." He sloped off at the end, running a hand through his unkempt green hair and looking pretty dejected.

"That was awful," said Harry slowly. "But there was also something weirdly familiar about it."

"I know," said Abby. "I'm sure I've heard some of those jokes before."

"Me too," said Harry. "But I can't think where."

"And I thought you two never bothered watching my old tapes," said a voice behind them.

"Dad!" said Harry and Abby, turning round. "What are you doing here?"

"Well, I'm on in about seventeen hours, so Mikey brought me here so I don't miss my cue," he said, chuckling, as Mikey smiled awkwardly behind him. "Anyway, look what I found."

Harry and Abby stared at the listening device that Gus put down in front of them.

"Another one," breathed Abby. "How could this have got into your pocket?"

"I'm not a hundred per cent certain," said Gus calmly. "But I'm guessing Nick put it there."

The twins gave each other a confused look.

"I actually *was* a bit suspicious after his last performance," said Gus. "So I did some research, and it turns out it's a listening device.

"No!" said Harry and Abby, feigning astonishment.

"Yes," went on Gus. "So after he came to see me earlier, I rehearsed some jokes that hadn't worked at all, really *terrible* stuff from the archives. Funny that he should then go and do the same material, isn't it?"

He smirked at Harry's and Abby's stunned expressions. "I'm not *entirely* stupid, you know."

The twins were about to assure their father that they didn't think that at all when they heard a shrill ringing. Tanya fumbled for her phone.

"Hello?" she barked. "What, *now*? OK, yes, I'll be there as soon as I can."

She turned to Harry, Abby and Rosy.

"I've got to pop off," she said. "Mikey can look after you all till I get back. Don't worry, though, I'll definitely be here for your big performance."

Harry and Abby inwardly groaned.

"I can't wait," Rosy said, grinning. "And don't worry. I can tell you're a bit nervous about it, but I know you'll be great."

"Thanks," said Harry and Abby together.

"Here's another odd thing," said Gus as Tanya went off. "Josie came up to me earlier. Told me not to worry; whatever happened, I would definitely be at the final. I mean, of course I will, but what's it got to do with her?"

"I wouldn't worry about it," said Harry as the lights dimmed.

The next act was Ali, the snake charmer. Harry and Abby could see her on the other side of the stage, waiting to go on.

Abby narrowed her eyes and scrutinized her as best she could. Ali was definitely still wearing a wig. Was this the moment she was going to unleash her plan? Abby braced herself for action.

"Are you OK about snakes now?" Harry whispered to Rosy.

"Totally fine. Erran's completely cured me," Rosy whispered back.

"Please welcome the most *charming* snake charmer in the world, Ali Saperas!" boomed Mac.

Ali entered carrying her basket, and almost immediately, Greta, who had been snoozing in Clive's lap, began barking and howling as if a cat had just appeared and told her she had a face like a blow-dried hamster with a runny nose.

"Oh dear," said Mac. "Something tells me the smell of snake doesn't quite agree with Greta."

Despite his best efforts, Clive couldn't get Greta to calm down, so he handed her to a woman on his make-up team who really didn't seem pleased to have been given a slobbering, barking creature to take out.

The disturbance didn't seem to affect Ali, though, and as she started playing her pungi, it became clear why Greta had gone quite so ballistic: this time she had *two* snakes. They rose up out of the basket and seemed to dance and intertwine to the raspy, high-pitched pipe music. The audience were utterly captivated, as were the judges, who raved about it.

"That was amazing," said Rosy as Ali came offstage on their side.

"Yes, congratulations," said Abby. "It was brilliant."

"Thank you," said Ali. "But wait and see what I have in store if I get to the final. It's REALLY special."

Abby smiled. *Ali does seem very nice*, she thought. *But why wear a wig? And what about Clive's keys? And what is the plan?*

"Hello, everyone, I'm back," said Tanya, bursting into Abby's thoughts. "Gus, you're on after the next act. Exciting!"

That act was Hot Dogs, the doggy dance troupe. They were huge favourites, and as Roisin marched them all out in sparkly disco doggy outfits, a massive cheer went up.

Their performance was incredibly skilful and adorably cute and as they danced around the stage to a medley of classic disco songs, everyone stood up, clapping and whooping. It was so much fun that Harry and Abby forgot to keep watch and relaxed, laughing and clapping like the rest of the audience.

That all changed very suddenly though when, halfway through the act, someone burst past Harry, Abby and the others and charged on to the stage.

"Spirit of Phompha," a voice wailed through a megaphone. "Forgive these people. They know not what they are doing! Lift the curse, lift the curse!"

It was Debbie. Her hair was now jet black and she

was wearing long, flowing white robes. Somehow, she had got past security, into the building and on to the stage.

"Do not destroy us all, oh great Phompha," she shouted. "Speak through me and we will listen to you."

It was carnage. The dogs were running around in their sparkly costumes, yapping and yelping like crazy. The audience were booing and shouting, and in the background a song called "Boogie Oogie Oogie" was still playing.

With so much going on, it took security quite a while to get to Debbie, but eventually they did and hauled her off. She had the last word, or rather words, though, which were, "Remember, my new series is on now!"

The show went straight to a break after that.

"How did she get in?" shrieked Tanya into her walkie-talkie. "How did she get past security?! Why didn't anyone stop her?!"

Tanya was clearly in quite a state, but, there was one question she didn't ask, and it was one, Harry and Abby imagined, that was probably troubling a lot of people – did Debbie Acorn really have supernatural powers that allowed her to contact a vengeful spirit called Phompha who was going to destroy everyone?

CHAPTER 20
Put to the Vote

"Thank you, everyone," said Gus, looking out at the crowd. "And for those of you concerned, I've just seen Debbie Acorn backstage. She's OK, though she does seem quite shocked. It's like she's seen a ghost."

The crowd liked that line.

"I loved the doggy dance troupe as well. Weren't their sparkly disco outfits fantastic? Bit naughty that they stole them from Mac's personal wardrobe, though."

The audience liked that one even more and roared with laughter. Mac laughed as well, though, thought Harry, possibly a bit too much. The show had restarted after the break with an apology for the disturbance during the Hot Dogs' performance and then they cracked straight on with Gus.

After those two jokes, Harry and Abby were relieved to see that the laughter stayed strong throughout. The judges' comments were all positive, though Clive was a little catty – "It was good, but was it good enough to get to the final? I'm not too sure." – and Gus walked off on the other side of the stage. The twins could see that he was immediately accosted by the behind-the-scenes crew, who were waiting to interview him.

"Your dad did really well, I don't think it'll be long now before you two are on," said Mikey as Mac introduced the next act, Girly Wirly.

"Can't wait," said Harry weakly. He looked around. "Where's Tanya?"

"Oh, she had to go off again," Mikey said.

"Really," said Harry, looking meaningfully at Abby.

"Abby, Harry," whispered Rosy. "How did Debbie get in? It's very strange. We need to investigate."

"There are lots of things I'd like to investigate," said Abby ruefully. "But we're stuck here."

Abby looked up. Onstage, the street dance act were nearing the end of their performance. On the other side of the stage, she could just see Mac waiting. She thought he seemed uptight and nervous. Could *he* have been responsible for getting Debbie in? It seemed absurd, but what if those conspiracy theories were right?

Abby kept her eyes on Mac as the street dance performance finished and he bounded back onstage. He was definitely in showbiz mode again as he asked the judges for their comments, sent the dancers off and then introduced the last act of the night, the acrobatic trio. After that, it was the public vote.

Mac told people they only had eight minutes to vote, which meant there was a lot of frantic activity as all the acts were gathered together, ready to go onstage for the result. At some point in the middle of it all, Tanya returned.

"Oh, hi, Tanya," said Harry, eyeing her suspiciously. "Where have you been?"

"Nowhere interesting," she said breezily. "Just dealing with production stuff."

"What kind of stuff?" said Harry.

"Boring stuff," said Tanya. "Now, are you both ready? It's almost time."

With that, she had shut down the conversation, and attention turned to the stage and Mac.

"OK, folks, the results are in, so let's welcome back all our semi-finalists!"

Rosy squealed as the acts trooped out and stood in a line awaiting their fate. Gus was at the end of the line with Mac to the right of him, on the other side of the stage. It was going to be a long run for Harry and Abby.

"OK, here we go," said Mac as the lights dimmed and a heavy blanket of tension descended. "In no particular order, the first act through to the final is . . . Ali Saperas!"

Ali's hands sprang to her mouth in shock. She'd made it.

One by one Mac read out the other acts who were through. Angie, Erran, the Hot Dogs, the BMX bikers and the acrobatic trio. That left just one space in the final.

Harry and Abby glanced at their father. It was

difficult to see clearly, but he seemed to have a look of supreme confidence on his face. If he was nervous, he was hiding it well.

"So, the line-up is almost complete, but there is room for one more act in the final. Good luck, everyone. The last act through to the final is. . ."

CHAPTER 21
Lies, Hugs and Bombshells

"...Girly Wirly!"

For a tiny moment an icy stalactite of silence hung in the air, but then the five members of the girl group collapsed in a heap on top of one another and the audience applauded wildly.

Harry and Abby looked at each other. Realization was dawning on them and with it, a weird mix of thoughts.

He hasn't got through, so we don't have to run onstage.

He hasn't got through, so how can we be here for the final?

He hasn't got through, Dad must be feeling really bad.

He hasn't got through . . . what do we do now?!

"Yes, I heard, all set," Tanya was saying into her

walkie-talkie. "Yes, they're still here, we're standing by."

"Oh no," said Rosy, really quite angrily. "That can't be right! There must be a mistake!"

Harry and Abby were looking at Gus. He was scratching his chin. He seemed lost and confused, and now they really did want to give him a hug.

"So we have our finalists," said Mac.

He paused. A long pause. This was unusual. A different type of silence radiated around the studio now. This one was expectant and curious.

"Or *do we*?" boomed Mac.

A rumble of surprise wriggled through the audience. Harry and Abby looked at each other. What was this all about?

"What's happening?" said Rosy.

"Shhh," said Tanya, smiling. "Listen."

"It seems that one of our finalists has been less than truthful," continued Mac.

Suddenly a spotlight burst on and shot around the stage before finally coming to rest on. . .

Angie!

She looked tiny in the glare of the light.

As one, the audience gasped.

"We were told that her family were very poor and she was doing this to give them a better life, but that isn't true, is it . . . Lady Monica Van Smedling Von Hockendoch?!"

Angie, or Lady Monica, put her head in her hands.

"The Von Hockendoch family have made a fortune from coat hangers and Lady Monica is the sole heir. She is worth millions!"

The audience gasped again and now a few boos rang out. Soon everyone was jeering and shouting.

"OK, OK," said Mac, gesturing for everyone to quieten down. "I'm afraid, my ladyship, because you lied to us, you have been disqualified!"

Cheers rang out as someone came on and led Lady Monica away.

"So that explains the expensive watch and the fancy car," whispered Abby.

"Yes," said Harry. "And I reckon her father was cross earlier because she sounded too posh when she was speaking onstage."

"Amazing what some families will do to become famous," said Abby.

Harry nodded. They both focused their attention back to the drama unfolding onstage.

"So, that means," said Mac, "we do *not* have all our finalists. There is still one place available, and that will go to the remaining act who received the next highest number of votes."

Rosy let out a yelp. She was clearly beside herself with excitement.

Harry and Abby glanced over at Gus. If anything, he looked even more confused now. He clearly hadn't followed what had been going on.

"So, here we go," said Mac. "The act with the next highest number of votes and through to the final is. . ."

Mac milked the moment for all it was worth. It was as if he was holding the audience in some sort of show-business cage which only he could open.

". . .Gus Moore!"

The audience went nuts as Mac ran over and stuck the microphone in Gus's face.

"Congratulations," he said. "You're through to the final. How are you feeling?"

"Well, I'm very pleased," spluttered Gus. They could

see that he was trying to think of something funny to say, but because of the turmoil and confusion, he was actually being genuine for once in his life. "I'm really, really pleased."

"Yay!" cheered Rosy from the side of the stage.

"Go, go, go," yelled Tanya.

At first Harry and Abby didn't realize she was talking to them, but then they felt a gentle hand on their backs propelling them forward.

They ran across the stage, keeping their eyes firmly focused on Gus the whole time. They were trying to tell him that after everything that had happened, they weren't going to do the comedy routine. They just wanted to give him a hug. Mercifully, for once, they were all on the same wavelength, and as the twins approached their father, he opened his arms and embraced them both. As the producers of the show had hoped, the audience loved it and roared their approval.

"Well," said Mac, wiping an imaginary tear away from his real eye. "Isn't that just beautiful? I guess they couldn't contain themselves. So, how do you feel about your dad getting to the final, young fella?"

Mac held the microphone out to Harry.

"I'm so happy," he said. "Mainly because I taught him everything he knows."

That got a big laugh.

"He's a real chip off the old block, isn't he, Gus?" said Mac.

"He is," said Gus proudly as he ruffled Harry's hair.

"And what about you, sweetheart?" said Mac to Abby. "How are *you* feeling about Dad making it to the final?"

There was a pause. For a moment you could hear a pin drop as the audience held their breath, waiting to hear what Abby would say.

She moved closer to the mic. "I'm not surprised he's gone through," she said, her voice loud and clear. "All the other contestants are second-rate losers who smell of cabbage and four-day-old farts."

KLUNK.

It was as if someone had poured a huge bucket of ice-cold water over the entire show.

That was *not* what anyone had been expecting.

CHAPTER 22
It's Time to Face the Music

"Boooooooooo! Boooooooooo! Boooooooooo!"

The atmosphere had changed in a second, as if someone had flicked a switch.

"All right, folks," said Mac, looking bewildered. "I'm sure she didn't mean it, she was just trying to be funny, weren't you, darling?"

Mac put the microphone in front of Abby again.

"I'm not surprised he's gone through. All the other contestants are second-rate losers who smell of cabbage and four-day-old farts," she said exactly as she had a moment ago. Harry was totally shocked. He looked at his sister in disbelief.

As a disconcerted Mac closed the show, the boos were still ringing out around the studio. Abby, Harry and Gus were hustled offstage by a stony-faced Tanya, who led them at speed to the secure staff area.

"What was *that* all about?" said Harry as they jogged after Tanya.

"Yes," said Gus. "It wasn't funny, it was just rude. Why did you say that?"

Abby swallowed. She was in shock. She wanted to cry, but she felt too confused.

"I, I really don't know," she said. "I didn't mean to, it . . . it just came out. I have no idea how or why."

"In here," snapped Tanya, opening the door to a room. "Josie wants to see you."

There was a table and a few chairs in the room, but that was it. They went in and waited. They sat in silence until there was a knock at the door and Josie entered.

"Thank you for waiting," she said formally. "I won't beat around the bush. As you can imagine, there has been a big public reaction to what happened.

Some people are suggesting you should also be disqualified, Gus."

Gus looked crestfallen and was about to say something when Josie continued.

"However," she said, looking pointedly at Gus, "I am not of that opinion, so you will be allowed to compete in the final. But Abby, as I'm sure you'll appreciate, we can't risk any more disruptive behaviour, so I'm afraid you won't be allowed to come to the studio for the final."

Abby nodded. She felt pretty devastated, but also very, very confused. She hadn't planned to say any of those things. What was going on?

"Is there anything you'd like to say?" said Josie.

"No, I . . . just that I didn't mean to do it," said Abby. "I don't know what happened."

"OK, well, we've prepared a press release," said Josie. "We're going to say that you were overcome by being onstage and thought you were being funny, but you realize now that what you said was wrong and hurtful, and you're very sorry. Is that OK?"

Abby nodded again.

"Good," said Josie. "I'm not sure how much that will

help but, well, we shall see. So, that's all. See you at the final, Gus."

Gus grunted something. It might have been "yes" or "bye" or "thanks", but it wasn't very clear.

"That's it, then," said Gus once Josie had left the room. "Not much point in me even turning up to the final; my chances of winning are practically zero now."

"Come on. Let's go," said Harry. He could sense Abby's discomfort and wanted to get her out of there as quickly as possible.

They hauled themselves up and headed off. A car was waiting for them and they were about to get in when Rosy came running up.

"Abby," she called. "What happened? Why did you say those things?"

"I don't know," said Abby miserably. "But I'm not allowed to come back. I'm sorry. See you."

She clambered into the car, leaving Harry to tell Rosy the news about the final.

"That's not fair," Rosy said, folding her arms defiantly. "I'm going to talk to Uncle Mac. He'll make them change their minds."

"I doubt it," said Harry. "But don't worry. I'll be there. We can catch the villain together."

"If you say so," said Rosy, looking at him dubiously.

They drove off with Rosy waving sadly.

It was late when they got home, so they all went to bed without further discussion. Sleep didn't come easily to Abby, though. She lay awake, staring at the ceiling.

None of this made sense. She was the one who liked to be in control and know what was going on. Upsetting people and making them angry were definitely not on her agenda. Above all, she had scuppered Gus's chances of winning – and she had no idea why.

The following morning, Abby went downstairs early. She had hoped to be alone, but not long after she'd popped two slices of bread in the toaster, Harry appeared.

"Good night's kip?" he said, a little too jauntily.

"Think I nodded off for about fifteen minutes," said Abby.

"Yup, me too," said Harry. "Hey, at least I was sort of right about Angie. Or Lady whatever her name is. And she's no longer a suspect, which is good, right?"

Harry was trying to find something that might edge Abby's mood up a little. It wasn't working.

The toast popped up, startling both of them.

"Erm, I wouldn't look online if I was you," said Harry.

"I wasn't going to," said Abby. "Look, I don't know why I said it. I didn't mean to. It just came out!"

Harry was about to reply when his phone rang. It was Trevor. He put him on speakerphone.

"Hi. It's Trevor," said Trevor.

"Yes, I know, your name came up on my phone," said Harry.

"Amazing," said Trevor. "Now listen, I need to speak to you alone. What on earth was your sister playing at yesterday? Has she completely lost her mind?"

"Hi, Trevor," said Abby. "You're on speakerphone."

"Oh, er, hi," said Trevor. "Just kidding. But what *did* happen yesterday?"

Abby shook her head. "I don't know," she said wearily. She was getting tired of saying it. "I can't explain it. Maybe I *did* lose my mind for a few minutes."

"Right, yes," said Trevor. "Anyway, the good news is, it doesn't really matter. The case is closed."

"What?!" blurted out the twins together.

"Yes," Trevor went on. "Debbie Acorn had her phone confiscated after she stormed the stage, and we found some *very* interesting messages on it. We traced the number to a producer called Tanya. She was the person who let her in because. . ."

". . .she was passed over for the senior producer's job," interrupted Abby.

"Exactly. And Debbie promised Tanya the senior producer's job on *her* show if she helped her get onstage."

"That would explain where Tanya went when we were at the side of the stage," said Harry. "She was letting Debbie in."

"Debbie will do anything for publicity," said Trevor darkly. "Even sabotage. She's been the one behind all of this – the accidents, the talking pet, the anonymous letters. Just so her spooky curse prophecy could be fulfilled."

"You know that for sure, do you?" said Harry. "You've got evidence?"

"Well, not yet, but we will. It all fits. Turning the

lights off, the sprinklers and the other things, they can all be traced back to someone working on *BBNS*. And that someone was Tanya."

"But people said *Josie* told them to do those things," said Harry.

"I have a theory about that," said Trevor. "Tanya worked closely with Josie. She could have recorded her at any time, spliced it together to sound like instruction and played it over the walkie-talkies. There you have it. And by the way, my theories are rarely wrong."

"I'm sure they're not," said Abby. "And how did they get into Clive's house to make the talking dog video?"

"Easy," said Trevor. "Producers are always going round to judges' houses to film segments for the show. Tanya could have pretended she needed the loo or something and just slipped off to film Greta. She might even have her own set of keys."

Abby had a flash of the keys she'd seen in Ali's handbag, but she decided not to say anything for the time being.

"All so that Debbie's show can get higher ratings," Trevor went on. "Show business is pretty cutthroat.

Anyway, my bosses are very pleased. And the palace is happy for a royal to attend the final now. In fact, I'm told they are rather excited. Who knows, I might get a knighthood for this. Sir Trevor Nibbleswick. Has a nice ring to it, don't you think?"

"Mmm," said Harry.

"Anyway, most importantly," said Trevor, "did you film my message from Gus?"

"Yes, we did it," said Harry.

Trevor almost squealed in delight. "What did he say? What did he say?" he shouted excitedly. "No, don't tell me. Just send it."

"We will," said Abby. "But what about our agreement? About Mum? You said you'd see what you could do to get her early release. . ."

"Ah," said Trevor. "I'm afraid that under the circumstances, that might be rather difficult. You see, I was hoping that you two would have solved this crime yourselves. Then I could have revealed that I recruited you and you would have come out of it very well. That would have made it easy to help with your mother. However, telling the world that you think the other contestants are rubbish, Abby, has made it considerably harder. People aren't exactly sympathetic to you, so, I'm sorry, but I just can't spare the time."

"But I didn't mean it," pleaded Abby. "Really."

"I'm sorry," said Trevor. "As I told you, the case is closed. There's nothing I can do."

CHAPTER 23

Rewind

BRITAIN'S BIGGEST NEW BRAT!

HAVING A LAUGH? NOT ANY MOORE!

YOU TWIN SOME, YOU LOSE THE LOT

These were just some of the headlines Abby would have seen had she chosen to look at the newspapers.

And there were others too.

ACORN ATTACK!

WOOOOOOOOOOOULD YOU BELIEVE IT?

DERANGED DEBBIE DISRUPTS DISCO DOGGIES

And, finally:

IT'S A YES FROM THE PRINCE

CROWNING GLORY: ROYAL TO ATTEND FINAL!

What with Abby's outburst, Debbie storming the stage and the royal prince confirmed as the special guest, *BBNS* fever had gripped the whole country. Ratings had shot through the roof and expectations for the final were sky high.

Sensibly, though, Abby had decided to ignore the headlines. Instead, after a morning of wallowing in misery and confusion, she decided it was time to fight back.

The turning point had come after she and Harry had started crying with laughter. As sometimes happens in difficult situations, something sets you off in the opposite direction. In this case it was when Harry said, "Four-day-old farts? Where did you conjure that up from?" Before they knew it, the two of them were rolling around on the floor, howling and clutching their stomachs.

"I needed that," said Abby, when she was able to speak again. "Right, enough is enough. Something fishy is going on. I didn't mean to say what I said last night. I'm going to find out what's going on."

"*We* are, you mean," said Harry.

Abby looked at her brother and smiled. "You believe me?" she asked.

"Of course," he said. "I know you're telling the truth. So what do we do?"

"You're not going to like it," said Abby. "We go back through everything that's happened, but in a planned, methodical way. No jumping around or silly jokes or crazy ideas. OK?"

"Yup," said Harry. "You got it."

"Let's start with Greta," said Abby. She brought up the clip which had kicked off this the whole mysterious business. Carefully, they listened to the dog predict a terrible curse in Clive's voice.

"Whoever did this, did a really good job," Abby said.

"Well, that makes me think it *was* Tanya," said Harry. "She's a TV producer and she had access to Clive's house."

Abby nodded. "Yeah, and she could have hired someone to do the voice. Or, if Trevor's theory is right, she could have recorded Clive herself and made it that way."

"Then the secret service are right," said Harry. "Debbie and Tanya were working together."

"Not so fast," said Abby. "There are other things to consider. If we take it in chronological order, there was that falling spanner."

"Yeah, that was really nasty," Harry said. "It could have decapitated poor Rosy."

"Tom seemed genuinely sorry and said it was an accident," said Abby. "But it could have been planned to spook people."

"Risky, but Tanya could have arranged that," said Harry. "And, going back to Trevor's theory again, she could also have arranged the whoopee cushions and everything that happened onstage."

"She could," said Abby. "And with her access-all-areas pass she could easily have got in to the gallery and switched the show's music on, and got into Eve's dressing room to write on her mirror."

"She'd also have all the addresses she'd need to send those threatening letters as well," added Harry. "It does seem to be pointing to her and Debbie."

"Maybe," said Abby. "But what about Tom giving

Erran his pass so that Erran could get into the staff area?"

"Yeah, that's definitely very suspicious," said Harry.

"And then there's Ali," Abby continued. "I overheard her saying that *everything was going to plan*. And she had Clive's keys in her bag."

"Also suspicious," said Harry. "Maybe she's working with Tanya and Debbie for some reason. And Tom and Erran. They could all be part of some big gang with Mac as the boss, if those conspiracy theories are true."

"I think you might be letting your imagination run away with you now, but there is definitely more that needs to be investigated and explained."

"Yes, erm, talking about that," said Harry. "There is one more thing to investigate."

"What?" said Abby nervously. She knew what was coming.

"Why you said what you said onstage," said Harry. "We need to watch it."

Abby shuddered. "I can't," she said. "I'm sorry. You'll have to do it on your own, Harry."

"OK," said Harry. "But I can't promise to do it methodically. I might stand on my head to watch it. Or run it backwards. Or eat a big plate of spaghetti at the same time."

"Fine," said Abby, standing up to leave the room. "Whatever you like, just do it."

So Harry watched it. He watched it again. And again. He did watch it eating spaghetti, then he watched it blindfolded so he could just hear the sound, then with the sound turned down and then, standing on one foot (he couldn't stand on his head).

Nothing made any difference, though. It played out the same way each time. Abby always said what she said. She looked like her normal self. It was *her* voice saying those words. She wasn't miming, she wasn't a robot, she wasn't a clone, she wasn't a hologram and she wasn't a puppet.

There was only one thing for it.

"I'm sorry, Abs," said Harry, calling her back in. "But I really think you should watch it yourself. I can't find anything."

Abby gritted her teeth. She'd thought that one day, maybe in twenty years' time, she might be brave enough to watch it again, but now? Today?

"It's not that bad, really," lied Harry.

Abby knew he was lying, but there was no other option. "Right then, let's get it over with," she said.

Harry hit the play button.

Abby's heart was pounding and her jaw was clenching her teeth so tightly, she thought they might fall out, but she kept watching as Mac announced Gus was through and the two of them charged across the stage.

She studied the screen, trying to remember how she'd felt. She'd been nervous. She'd known Mac was going to speak to her after he'd spoken to Harry, so she was thinking about what to say. *I'm really happy Dad has got to the final, he's done brilliantly*, is what she'd planned to say.

She leaned forward, watching intently as Mac asked her how she felt about her dad getting to the final.

"I'm not surprised he's gone through. All the other contestants are second-rate losers who smell of cabbage and four-day-old farts," said Abby.

But she hadn't just said the words on the computer screen. At the very same moment Abby had said the exact same words, there and then in the house.

CHAPTER 24
Definitely Not Getting Sleepy

The twins froze.

"What . . . what did you say?" asked Harry.

Abby stared at him. "The words just came out. I couldn't stop myself."

"Hang on a minute," said Harry.

He played the clip again, and sure enough, at the exact moment when Mac put the microphone to Abby's mouth, the same thing happened. Abby repeated the words she'd said onstage.

The two of them looked at each other.

"I've been hypnotized!" said Abby.

"You've been hypnotized!" said Harry.

"Of course," said Abby. "It makes sense now. Somehow Erran must have hypnotized me."

"And he didn't see you afterwards," said Harry, picking up where Abby left off. "So he wasn't able to snap you out of it, that's why you did it again just now. But how did he know we were on to him?"

Abby thought for a moment. "It was Erran who gave me back my microphone after I was knocked over by that dog. And I'm guessing he *did* see you in the toilet. And Rosy worked it out, so maybe we aren't the best undercover spies in the world. . ."

"I guess," said Harry. "So he must have hypnotized Tom to give him an access-all-areas pass. Then he was able to get to Josie and hypnotize her to give out all those instructions."

"It seems so, yes," said Abby.

"OK, but that leaves one question," said Harry. "Why? Why did he do it?"

"Well," said Abby, "as a result of him hypnotizing me, I got banned from the studio. No more snooping around and investigating. So the short answer is, we must have got too close to Erran for his liking."

"But what about me?" said Harry. "I'm just as much of an investigative threat."

"I think he was sending us both a message," said Abby. "He's telling us that he's got rid of me, so he can get rid of you any time he wants to as well. He must think we'll back off now."

"No chance," said Harry. "But why does he want to sabotage the whole show?"

"I don't know," said Abby. "I think we'll have to do some digging and see what we can find out about him. But first, play the clip again."

"Are you sure?" said Harry. "He may have hypnotized you to explode if you watch it too many times."

"I'll take that risk," said Abby. "I want to watch Erran this time."

Harry put the clip on again with the sound down.

"There. Look at Erran's face," said Abby.

Harry rewound it and sure enough, as Abby spoke, a small but obvious smirk spread across Erran's face. It wasn't easy to see, but if you looked closely, there was no doubt about it.

"We need to tell Trevor," said Abby. "They might have arrested the wrong people."

"I'll call him," said Harry, grabbing his phone.

"Hello," said Trevor.

"Agent 4905-3, it's Harry, I need to talk to you."

"Harry, if this is about your mother again, then I'm sorry, but I made it clear—"

"It's not," interrupted Harry. "We've worked out what happened. Abby was hypnotized by Erran; he's the real villain. Tanya did let Debbie in, for publicity for Debbie's show, but they didn't do the other things, he did!"

"Harry, there will always be conspiracy theories," said Trevor. "I saw one earlier suggesting that Greta and Eve's goldfish were behind everything. It's ludicrous, a fish can't stay out of water for more than a few seconds. Now, as I told you yesterday, the case is closed."

"But Trev . . . Agent 49. . ."

"Actually, I'm already on my next case," continued Trevor, ignoring Harry. "A very hush-hush one involving illegal toilet smuggling . . . oops, shouldn't have mentioned that, keep it to yourself. Now look, one last thing. That film of your father you sent me, I know you're not professional, but there's a lot of noise and Abby and that Ruby girl are milling around in the background too."

"Rosy," corrected Harry glumly.

"Yes, her," said Trevor. "Anyway, I suppose it will have to do. Got to go now, lots of work to do on Operation Lulu."

He hung up. The twins looked at each other.

"So now what?" said Harry.

"There's really only one other person left to contact," said Abby. "Josie."

"Yes, of course," said Harry. "What's her number?"

"I haven't got it," said Abby. "But I'll bet Rosy can get it from Mac."

Harry immediately got on the phone to Rosy, who was very happy to hear from the twins.

"But I thought the case was closed," she said. "Uncle Mac said that Tanya and Debbie are under arrest."

"We think they've got the wrong people," said Abby. "We think Erran is involved. We need to speak to Josie."

"Uncle Mac will definitely have her number," Rosy

said. "I'll borrow his phone. He lets me play games on it sometimes when my battery runs out. My favourite is Liquorice Lobster, but I also like Style My Seagull."

"Great," said Abby. "As soon as you get the number, can you send it to us?"

"OK," said Rosy. "And Abby, I knew you wouldn't say those horrible things, but why did Erran do it, and why does he want to ruin the show?"

"I don't know," said Abby. "That's what we're going to try and find out. Whatever the reason, though, we have to speak to Josie and stop him."

"Don't worry," said Rosy. "I'm on it. Bye."

For the first time in what seemed like ages, Harry and Abby stopped for a moment and sat in contemplative silence, letting their brains take stock of everything until they were jolted out of it by the clang of the letterbox.

"I'll go," said Harry getting up. He returned holding an A4 envelope.

"This came for you," he said, handing it to Abby.

Abby took the envelope. "What could it be?" she said, frowning.

254

A couple of moments later she knew exactly what it was.

You were getting in my way, you foolish dolt.

Now you are gone and nothing can stop me.

Sit at home and watch as I bring the final to a memorable climax that will result in the end of Britain's Biggest New Star . . . for ever!

Ha ha ha ha ha ha ha ha ha ha ha

Terrifying as it was, the letter proved one thing. The twins were right; the real villain was definitely still out there.

CHAPTER 25

Revenge

"Careful," said Harry. "Erran might have done something to the letter so that it hypnotizes you again."

"I don't think that's how it works," said Abby, looking at the envelope. This one had a UK postmark. "But it has made me even more determined to catch him. It's time to do some digging."

Hunched over the computer together, Harry and Abby searched for "Erran Clark Hypnotist". There was a lot of information – he had his own website, there were reviews of past shows he'd done and of course, lots of information in the news about how he was doing on *BBNS* – but nothing incriminating. They then searched various combinations of words such as "Erran Clark Hypnotist Criminal", "Erran Clark Hypnotist Controversy", "Erran Clark Hypnotist Evil Wizard" (that was Harry's idea) and "Erran Clark Hypnotist Angry", but they were all dead ends.

Next, they tried searches linking him to the show, such as "Erran Clark Hypnotist BBNS" or "Erran Clark Hypnotist Talent Show". They didn't bear fruit either.

It was proving to be quite a thankless task, but then Harry had a brainwave.

"Remind me what Wally's surname is again," he said.

"Deighton," said Abby.

Harry typed in "Erran Clark Hypnotist Wally Deighton".

There were lots of results, mainly to do with the current show, until eventually...

"Boom," shouted Harry. "Gotcha. You messed with the wrong twins, Mr Clark!"

"What is it?" said Abby.

"Well," said Harry. "It seems that some years ago,

Erran wanted Wally Deighton to be his agent, but Wally didn't take him on."

Harry turned the computer so that Abby could see the screen. There it was, clear as day, a post on Erran's social media.

Got turned down by Wally Deighton's talent agency today. Gutted.

"Wow," said Abby. "Do you really think that's it?"

"It must be," said Harry. "And it was years ago, so all that anger has been building up and Erran's finally cracked. He wants revenge."

Harry was holding his hand up to high-five Abby when her phoned pinged. It was a message from Rosy with Josie's number.

"I think it would be better if *you* called her," Abby said. "I'm not exactly her favourite person at the moment. Do it now."

Harry took a deep breath and called the number. Josie answered after three rings.

"Hi, Josie, it's Harry."

"Harry?" said Josie. "What's up? There's nothing wrong with Gus, is there?"

Harry was tempted to say that there were a *lot* of things wrong with Gus, but he didn't. Instead he told Josie about Erran's connection to Wally and their discovery about Abby being hypnotized.

"Hypnotized?" said Josie. "What on earth. . ."

"I know it sounds crazy," said Harry quickly. "But it's the only thing that makes sense of all this. We couldn't work out why Erran kept sneaking into the secure staff area – but this explains why. We've all seen what he makes people to do. He could have hypnotized you to tell someone to turn the lights off during the knife-throwing act. And all the other things. He could have hypnotized someone to let him into Clive's house as well, to make the pet video."

"OK," said Josie a little uncertainly. "But why would he hypnotize Abby?"

Harry stopped. He remembered that Josie didn't know about him and Abby working for the secret service.

"Erm, well, you see, because of everything that's been going on, we've sort of been doing some investigating of our own," he said.

"What?" said Josie, startled.

"Yeah. And we saw Erran getting a pass off Tom and going into the secure staff area, so we followed him and I'm pretty sure he saw us. Well, me. And so he hypnotized Abby to get her kicked out of the studio and scare us both off."

There was a long silence. "So, you're saying, he's had a grudge against Wally and the show for years, and that's why he's trying to scupper it, to get his own back," said Josie.

"Absolutely. If you watch the moment Abby speaks onstage, he definitely smirks. It's as clear as day."

There was another silence. "Do you believe us?" Harry said at last.

"Well," said Josie slowly, "it does have a certain logic... OK, I'll check the tape and look into what you've said. And if – *if* – I think there's more to this, I'll have security bring Erran in and interview him."

Harry let out a sigh of relief. That was about as good as could be expected, he thought. "Sounds like a plan," he said. "Thanks for listening."

"I just hope this isn't a wild goose chase," said Josie. "I've got a million things to do before the final. Bye."

Harry hung up.

"That sounded positive," said Abby. "What's the plan?"

"She's going to have security interview Erran," Harry said. "She didn't laugh at me, at any rate."

"Thank goodness," said Abby.

"Thank goodness indeed." The voice came from behind them.

"Muuuuum!" shouted Harry and Abby.

"There's no need to shout," said Mum. "I'm right next to you."

"But that's exactly it!" said Abby. "You shouldn't be. Oh, Mum, at this rate you'll never get out."

"I'm out now, aren't I?" said Mum.

"You know what I mean," snapped Abby, though secretly she was happy to see her mother.

Samantha gave them both a big hug. As they snuggled in, they relaxed a little for the first time in ages.

"Now," said Samantha. "Why don't you tell me what's going on?"

The twins explained everything to Samantha, who listened intently.

"Well, that's a relief," she said, when they'd finished.

"A relief?" said Abby.

"Yes," their mother went on. "I watched the show and knew that something was up. I wasn't sure you'd be able to deal with the fallout, but now I see you're made of strong stuff. Unlike your father. You must get it from me."

"You watched the show?" said Harry.

"Of course," said Samantha. "I watched it in the prison governor's office. Although he doesn't know, so don't tell him."

The twins shook their heads in disbelief.

"So, this Josie person," went on Samantha. "You sure she's OK?"

"What do you mean?" said Abby, a sense of panic rising up in her.

"Well," said Samantha. "That's some pretty important information you've just handed over to her."

"Oh, Mum," said Harry breezily. "You've been in prison too long. Not everyone's a criminal, you know."

"Mmm, OK," said Samantha, glancing at Abby.

She stayed another few minutes, just time for a

quick cuppa and to give the twins a very important message about looking for a button that had fallen off a blouse of hers six years ago. Then, as per usual, she upped and left.

"Well," said Harry. "It's in Josie's hands now. What do you think she's going to do?"

"I guess we'll find out," said Abby. "All we can do now is sit tight and wait for the final. . ."

CHAPTER 26

The Final

"Dad, they're calling you," said Harry. "Come on."

It was the day of the final and Gus had just been called for a rehearsal. The whole place was buzzing. Loads of celebrities were expected for the show and of course the royal prince would be there. Everyone was charged, hyped, pumped and exhilarated. Everyone, that is, apart from one person.

"What's the point?" said Gus glumly. "Abby's turned everyone against me. They think it's all my fault. 'Worst parent ever' was trending again last night."

"Dad," said Harry. "Trust me, I'm certain people

will change their minds about that. Anyway, you said you'd give it your best shot."

"This *is* my best shot," replied Gus, scowling. "You can tell them I'm not coming."

The only thing Gus was likely to win in this state was Britain's Biggest Sulker. Harry sighed and went to tell the rehearsal producer that Gus wasn't feeling well. Wandering back, Harry was thinking how to snap Gus out of his misery when he heard a familiar voice.

"Gussy, baby! How are things?"

It was Mac. His entourage of show staff were with him, along with Rosy, who raised her eyebrows meaningfully at Harry.

"Schnorbitz," she whispered.

For a moment Harry didn't know what she meant, but then he remembered their code words. She needed to talk.

"Oh, hi, Mac," said Gus, not even bothering to slip into showbiz mode.

"Hey, why the long face?" said Mac. "It's never over till it's over. You know what they say: when the going gets tough, the tough get going."

How many clichés could one man trot out? Harry thought. Rosy jerked her head and the two of them snuck away.

"Did you speak to Josie?" said Rosy.

"Yes, I did," said Harry. "She said she'd be getting security to speak to Erran. Hopefully they've already done that and he's now in a police cell somewhere."

"Erm, I don't think so," said Rosy. "I just saw him."

"What?" said Harry, frowning. Had Josie changed her mind? Maybe Erran had convinced her he was innocent. Or maybe he'd hypnotized her again.

"Yes. In fact," whispered Rosy, "there he is."

Harry looked up. Sure enough, Erran *was* there, and he and Ali the snake charmer were both heading towards Gus.

"We need to find out what he's up to," said Harry. "And be careful. He might try and hypnotize someone else. Whatever you do, Rosy, don't look at his eyes."

Harry and Rosy rushed back. To Harry's horror, even though Mac was still talking to Gus, Gus was looking directly at Erran. Harry barged in and gave his

266

father a big hug, putting his face right in front of Gus's and keeping it there.

"Whoa, that's some big love you're getting there from Henry," said Mac. "At least you've still got one fan left! See you later, and good luck."

Harry had practically glued his face to Gus's now, but he couldn't find the words to go with his actions, so he just stayed there. It was all very awkward.

"Erm," said Erran, looking at Harry and Gus in confusion. "We just came over to wish you good luck, and tell you about our new business venture."

"Oh yes?" said Gus, though it was more of a mumble, as a large part of Harry's face was covering his mouth.

"Yes," said Ali, ploughing on as if nothing odd was happening. "A lot of people get scared of the snakes in my act, so in future, if anyone does, Erran is going to come out onstage and cure them. Like a sort of double act."

Gus managed to prise Harry away long enough to say, "That sounds terrific," but almost as soon as he'd done it, Rosy jumped in and smothered him in an enormous hug.

"Well, erm, you seem to have your hands full at the moment," said Erran. "We'll see you later. Good luck again."

Erran and Ali went off. "What on earth is going on with those kids?" Harry heard Ali say.

"Yeah. What on earth is going on?" said Gus.

"I can't explain now," said Harry. "But I will, I promise. Just stay here and if Erran comes back . . . put a paper bag over your head. Come on, Rosy."

"Where are we going?" said Rosy, as they scurried away.

"We're going to follow Erran," said Harry. "Something's not right. He's far too relaxed. He must think he's going to get away with it."

"Look," said Rosy, pointing.

Harry looked up just as Erran was going past security again. He must have already hypnotized Tom to give him his pass again.

Thankfully, the security guards hadn't forgotten who Rosy's uncle was, so she and Harry quickly slipped past them and scoured the corridor and surrounding area looking for Erran.

It wasn't easy, though. With the prince arriving later, there were extra security personnel everywhere, and the regular show staff were charging about all over the place. It was like a beehive during rush hour and, search as they might, they couldn't see Erran anywhere.

"What now?" said Rosy, looking up at Harry hopefully.

"I don't know," said Harry. "I don't know."

He felt confused and frustrated. In his mind everything should have been sorted by now. What was going on? Then he saw Josie heading towards the production office.

"Actually, I *do* know," he said firmly. "Come on."

Rosy followed as Harry hurried off.

"Josie! Josie," Harry shouted.

Josie turned round, along with everyone else in the corridor, which made Harry feel very self-conscious.

"Harry? What are you doing back here?" she said.

"I really need to speak to you," said Harry. "It's important."

"Harry, look," said Josie, her expression sympathetic.

"If this is about your sister, then I'm sorry, but there's nothing I can do. It's best if she lies low for a while."

Harry dropped his voice. "It's not. It's about Erran," he said quietly.

Josie looked blankly at him. "Erran?" she said. "The hypnotist?"

"Yeah. You know," he said. "You told me you would look into it after we spoke the other day? On the phone?"

"I'm sorry, Harry. I have no idea what you're on about," said Josie. "Now I really have to get on. Maybe see you after the show."

Harry stared after her.

"I don't understand," said Rosy.

"Neither do I," said Harry. "We need to call Abby."

"That is very odd," said Abby after Harry had told her what had happened. "Unless . . . that's it! She's been hypnotized already! Erran got to her before you could."

"Yes, that must be it!" said Harry. "But how did Erran know we'd spoken to Josie?"

"Because she told him, of course," said another voice on the phone.

"Mum?" said Harry.

"Oh sorry, forgot to tell you," said Abby. "Mum's come home to watch the final because her cellmate wants to watch something on another channel. Go on, Mum."

"She's totally in his power," said Samantha. "He must have hypnotized her to tell him everything, then wiped her memory. You've seen his act. In the semifinal, as well as making Wally hiccup, he made that woman from the audience think she was an ostrich, an elephant, a donkey and then a caterpillar. All with a click of his fingers."

Mum was right. It would be easy for Erran to control Josie. But perhaps he wasn't doing this on his own.

"Erran and Ali told us they're going into business together," said Harry. "Maybe they planned this together because Wally also turned Ali down in the past."

"It's possible," said Abby. "What exactly did they say about going into business together, Harry? ... Harry? ... Harry?"

Harry didn't answer Abby because he'd just seen a cleaner walk past him in overalls.

Only, it wasn't a cleaner.

It was Erran.

CHAPTER 27

The Corridor of Uncertainty

"I've just seen Erran," whispered Harry into the phone. "Dressed as a cleaner. I'm going after him."

"Be careful," said Abby. "He could be dangerous."

"Don't worry," said Harry. "I will be. Bye."

"I'm coming with you," said Rosy as Harry put the phone away.

"No, Rosy," said Harry. "I don't think that's a good idea. If something happens to both of us, there'll be no one to alert security. Go back to Dad and wait. If I need help, I'll text 'Bluebottle'. OK?"

"OK," said Rosy, looking concerned. "But there isn't going to be any trouble, is there, Harry?"

"I'll be fine," he said. "See you later."

Harry set off, glancing at his phone. Only three per cent battery left. He wished he'd charged it before they'd left home that morning, but there wasn't much he could do about it now. He had a hypnotist to follow.

Despite all the people around, Harry kept his gaze fully focused on Erran, who was doing his best not to draw attention to himself. He was wearing a cap pulled down low over his eyes and keeping his head down.

But where *was* he going?

Harry followed as Erran turned off the main corridor on to a quieter one. At the end he went up a flight of stairs and then along another corridor. There were fewer people around now, so Harry had to be more careful, but he didn't lose sight of his target.

Erran went up another three flights of stairs until he got to the top floor. There only seemed to be one very long corridor up there, so Harry hung back a little. When he stuck his head round the corner, the corridor was empty.

Erran had to be in one of the rooms off it. The first door Harry came to was locked. The next three were also locked. There was only one room left, at the farthest end of the corridor. Harry edged along the wall until he came to the door. Right in the middle of it was a big gold star with the words MAC TATUM written inside. It was Mac's dressing room. And the key was in the door.

Harry stopped. He hadn't realized how nervous he was. He was breathing like a hair dryer set to superfast and his heart was performing an insane beatbox routine.

"Calm down," he said to himself, taking deep breaths.

It took a few moments, but eventually he began to feel more in control. He'd already decided on his cover story. If Erran confronted him, he'd say Rosy had said to meet him there. As to what might happen next . . . well, Harry would just have to deal with it as best he could.

He took one last deep breath, gripped the door handle, and pushed.

The first thing Harry noticed was how luxurious the room was. There was a huge leather sofa, a plush rug, a giant television and a table groaning with fruit, snacks and drinks. There were also eight vases full of flowers, a dressing table covered in lotions, creams and sprays, and a pile of magazines that almost reached the ceiling.

What there wasn't, though, was any sign of Erran.

Harry looked around and saw another door. It must lead to the bathroom. It was the only place Erran could be. Harry was creeping towards the door when suddenly he heard a sound behind him. He swung round to see Erran coming out of a cupboard. He looked confused.

"What are you doing here?" said Erran. "You're not Mac."

"No," said Harry. "Neither are you. What are *you* doing here?"

"I came to see him," said Erran.

"Did you now?" said Harry. He steeled himself. "So you could hypnotize him?"

"Yes," said Erran.

"Oh," said Harry, a little taken aback. "Um. Just like you hypnotized Tom to give you his pass and Josie to give those instructions and Abby to say those rude things?"

"What?" said Erran, looking confused.

"All so you could sabotage the show and get your own back on Wally because he turned you down all those years ago. Yeah, we're on to you."

"I don't know what you're talking about," said Erran. "I *am* here to hypnotize Mac – for my act. Tom is an old friend. He gives me his pass so I can get into the staff area, disguise myself as a cleaner and get in to the stars' dressing rooms. Then I pre-hypnotize them. Before the show."

"Pre-hypnotize?" said Harry, looking blank.

"Yes," went on Erran. "That way they're already hypnotized when I come on, so I just have to say their name and they do whatever I've told them to do straight away. I was going to get Mac to pretend to be a baby."

"Really?" said Harry.

"Yes," said Erran. "I didn't hypnotize Tom. Or Josie. Or Abby. And yeah, Wally turned me down years ago, but it was no big deal. Really."

Harry gathered himself. "No, you're lying! We watched the tape back. You smirked when Abby said all that stuff."

"I did, yes," said Erran. "I couldn't help myself. I could tell she'd been hypnotized *and* she'd just ruined Gus's chances of winning. Someone had done me a big favour. But I promise you, Abby wasn't hypnotized by me."

Harry looked at Erran. He didn't seem to be lying. Harry had an uncomfortable feeling that maybe they'd got it wrong.

"So, who *did* hypnotize Abby?" said Harry.

Erran frowned. "I don't know," he said, "but—"

THWUNK!

The door to Mac's dressing room had been slammed shut and they both heard the key turning in the lock.

"Thought you could stop me, did you?" said a deep voice from outside. "You fools. You won't be going anywhere now. Mac won't be back here till after the show. And by that time, Britain's Biggest New Star – and the prince – will be the laughing stock of the world! Enjoy the show!"

Harry and Erran looked at each other as they heard footsteps walking away from the room. Harry rattled the door handle – but there was no doubt about it. They were trapped.

There was no doubt about something else either – the identity of who had locked them in. The broad Scottish accent was very distinctive.

It was the producer, Josie.

CHAPTER 28

Flu Bugs and Rug Rats

"What do we do now?" asked Erran.

Harry took a deep breath. "Don't panic," he said, taking out his phone. "I'll call Abby."

Abby picked up right away. "Harry, are you all right?" she said.

"Yes. And no," said Harry. "I'm trapped in Mac's dressing room with Erran."

"What?" shouted Abby. "Don't let him hypnotize you."

"Don't worry, he won't," said Harry. "But listen, we've been locked in by . . . hello? Hello? Oh no!"

Harry's phone had died.

"Quick, Erran, give me your phone," he said.

"I don't have it," said Erran. "It's in my jacket, which is in the cleaners' room."

Harry looked at Erran. They both knew what this meant. They were trapped in a room as far away from everyone else as it was possible to be. They didn't have a phone. The door was locked and there were no windows. It seemed it was game, set and match to Josie. Whatever it was she was planning, it wasn't looking good for the show – or the prince.

Harry and Erran spent the next twenty minutes banging and shouting on the door and trying to pick the lock. Neither were successful.

"I don't think anyone's going to find us," said Erran, resigned to their fate.

"No," said Harry. "And even if Abby has contacted the studio to raise the alarm, Josie will have stopped anyone taking it seriously."

"Why on earth does Josie want to scupper her own show?" said Erran, bewildered.

Harry sighed. "I think she's working undercover for a rival network," he said.

"Right," said Erran. "Hey, at least we've got a telly."

"Yeah," said Harry, sitting down and flicking on the TV. It seemed so unfair to have come this far only to watch their failure unfold on television.

The show opened with an amazing burst of lights and pyrotechnics. Mac was in a white tuxedo and beamed as he bowed to the royal box and welcomed the prince before introducing the judges.

"Now, before we crack on with our first act, I have an announcement," he said. "Unfortunately our hypnotist, Erran, has been taken ill and won't be able to perform."

Harry and Erran looked at each other and raised their eyebrows. The audience gave a collective groan.

"I know, I know," continued Mac. "But these things happen. Erran, get well soon, mate, and maybe work on hypnotizing those flu bugs in future. But the show must go on and it will – with our first act of the night, Mr Gus Moore!"

"Oh no," groaned Harry. Gus had been so miserable, Harry couldn't imagine him making much of an effort. He even thought Gus might not show up.

As it turned out, Gus, ever the professional, did make an effort. He even used what had happened with Abby in his act – "I was shocked by what my daughter said. I never knew she could be so opinionated, blunt and uncaring, though on the plus side, when she grows up, she'll make a great politician" – but the laughs weren't belly laughs and the applause at the end was lukewarm. Harry felt for him, but at least he'd tried.

The next act was Girly Wirly. The audience loved them.

"They'll probably win," Erran said bitterly.

"Maybe," said Harry. "But I'm sure you could have as well."

Harry was trying to be kind, but he didn't know if that would make Erran feel worse. He was fretting about it in his head when something very strange happened by his feet; Mac's rug started to move.

"Erran! Look!" Harry shouted.

Erran jumped up. "It must be one of Ali's snakes!" he screeched.

"I'm not a snake," said a voice. "Now, get this rug off me."

Despite the voice being a little muffled, Harry recognized it straight away. With help from Erran, they heaved the rug to one side to reveal. . .

Mum!

Her head was poking through a hole in the floorboards, and just behind her was another head.

Abby!

Harry and Erran hauled them into the room.

"Am I pleased to see you two," said Harry.

"But why didn't you use the front door?"

"Pah, too easy," said Samantha.

"And, as it's me," said Abby, "they might not have let us in. Plus we didn't want whoever locked you in this room to know we're here."

"Good thinking. Oh, sorry," said Harry, noticing Erran staring in utter bewilderment. "Erran, this is my mum; Mum, this is Erran. He's a hypnotist."

"Hi," said Erran "Nice to meet you. Er. How did you. . .?"

"Oh, Mum is something of an expert at getting in and out of places," said Harry. "But actually, how did you manage to find us here?"

"Well, I had a good look round when I visited the studio before," said Mum.

Harry gave his mother a quizzical look.

"Might have touched a few buttons I shouldn't have as well," said Mum.

"Surely you've figured it out," said Abby. "That time someone was in the gallery? The music playing?"

"You're kidding," said Harry. "That was you? Of course, that smell, it was your perfume."

Samantha grinned. Illegally breaking in to a television gallery and fiddling with the equipment was an odd way to impress your children, but she still felt a surge of pride.

"OK," said Harry. "There's no time to lose. It was

Josie all along. She locked us in here. We've got to get to her quickly, she's planning to do something to the prince."

"Josie?" said Abby. "No way. She seems so sensible."

"It was definitely her," Harry said. "We both heard her, clear as anything."

Erran nodded in agreement. "One hundred per cent," he said. "I'd swear to it."

"OK," said Abby. "She spends most of her time in the gallery. Mum, can you get us there?"

Mum made a face that said, *Of course I can*, and then the four of them squeezed into the hole in the floorboards.

The gallery was back on the ground floor and they had to crawl along and down a maze of pipes, rafters and ledges to get there. Eventually, though, they found themselves by an air vent.

"This opens out into the gallery," whispered Mum. "Bit of a squeeze. Are you sure you're ready for this?"

Harry and Abby looked at each other.

"Let's do it," they said together.

CHAPTER 29
A Lot of Venting

Abby kicked off the cover, and she and Harry tumbled out and on to the floor of the gallery. They landed with quite a thump.

As one, a row of producers, production assistants, sound engineers, vision mixers and the director turned to look at them, their faces a mixture of shock and disbelief. A moment later, they all experienced the same emotions again when Mum and Erran slid out and landed next to the twins.

"Josie!" gasped Harry, staggering to his feet. "We know it was you. *You're* the person who's been sabotaging the show. You're under arrest!"

BANG!

There was a stunned silence. Behind them, on one of the television screens, Ali was beginning her snake-charming act.

"What are you talking about?" cried Josie with such force the headset she was wearing almost flew off. "We're in the middle of the show. I'm calling security!"

"She locked me and Harry in Mac's dressing room," said Erran quickly.

"And said the show and the prince would be the laughing stock of the world!" shouted Harry.

"Have you gone crazy?" said Josie. "I've been here or the production office all day. I haven't been near Mac's dressing room."

"I can vouch for that," said the director.

"And me," said a production assistant.

"Thank you," said Josie. "Now, we're trying to produce the biggest live show on television, so you four stay there and keep quiet or. . ."

Josie stopped. Her eyes widened so much her eyebrows were almost touching her hair. Everyone else followed her gaze to the screen showing Ali.

She'd been performing. This time she not only had a

snake, she also had a small dog, a rabbit, a tortoise and a parrot, all of which she had been expertly controlling with her pungi. As they watched, though, Ali stopped and laid down her pungi. The animals all waited quietly as she walked to the front of the stage.

"Wide shot, camera four," shouted Liz, the director.

"There's something I need to tell you all," Ali said, her voice carrying in the astonished silence. "I'm not who you think I am."

Everyone in the gallery could now see the judges looking bemused as Ali took off her glasses. Then, to gasps of amazement from the audience, she tugged off her thick mane of black hair, revealing much shorter light brown hair underneath.

Clive Derek let out a yelp and pushed back his chair. Ali stepped forward.

"That's right, Clive," Ali said. "Greta recognized me in the semi-final. Do *you* recognize me now?"

Clive was on his feet. "Aditi," he said. His usually cheerful face was flushed and startled. "I don't believe it."

Josie snapped into action. "Get over there, Mac," she shouted into a microphone.

Mac, who had been standing staring, bounded over to Aditi.

"Well, this is unexpected," he said. "It seems you two are . . . old friends?"

"Not exactly," said Aditi. "I'm an animal trainer. Clive hired me to house-train Greta."

"Did you now, Mr Derek?" said Mac.

"I did," said Clive. "But, er, I had to let Aditi go. It wasn't working out."

"You fired me because you didn't think I was doing a good job!" snapped Aditi.

"Well, that's one way of putting it, yes," said a slightly embarrassed Clive.

"Then you told all your friends I was rubbish and *they* fired me too! You destroyed my reputation."

"Ah, now, you see. . ." Clive started to say, but Aditi swept on.

"All because you couldn't be bothered to use my techniques. Techniques I've been using successfully for years!"

Clive had given up making excuses. He looked like a naughty little boy who'd been caught stealing sweets.

"Sorry," he said.

"So I decided to show you what a good animal trainer I really am," continued Aditi, smiling triumphantly.

"You certainly proved that," said Mac. "Didn't she, Clive?"

"She did," said Clive humbly. "Aditi, I was wrong to fire you. I apologize. I was too busy to do your exercises. I wish I had, though; it would have stopped Greta weeing on my rug. And my bed. And, on one occasion, an entire basket of clean laundry."

The audience laughed.

"Aditi, please come back," said Clive. "I've only got two clean shirts left."

Clive went onstage and embraced Aditi, who was beaming. The audience applauded wildly.

"And," said Clive directly into the camera, "to all my friends. Rehire Aditi. Now!"

"You can come and train my goldfish any day," shouted Eve.

"Yeah!" cried Diamond punching the air, as Wally looked on with a wide grin on his face.

"Wow," said Aditi. "Even if I don't win, I feel like a winner already," she said.

"Well, that's the first time anyone's been so happy to get a job working for Clive," quipped Mac. "Let's hear it one more time for Ali – or rather, Aditi – the snake charmer!"

The audience roared as Aditi walked offstage with the snake in its basket, the parrot on her shoulder and the rabbit, dog and tortoise trooping obediently along by her side.

"Well done," said Josie, sounding relieved. "Go to a break, for goodness' sake."

She glanced around and saw that Harry, Abby, Samantha and Erran were still standing there.

"Right, you lot, out," snapped Josie. "We can discuss this nonsense later."

"No, listen," said Abby. "Something's not right. Someone locked Erran and Harry in Mac's dressing room. I was hypnotized to say what I said onstage. And that's not even counting the threatening letters."

"What?" shouted Josie. "How do you know about that?"

"We were hired by the secret service," said Harry. "We're working undercover for them."

"The secret service are hiring thirteen-year-olds?" said one of the producers, saying pretty much what everyone was thinking.

"If this is some sort of joke," said Josie, shaking her head.

"It isn't. We also know about you working for them because of your uncle," said Abby.

That did it for Josie; she looked both startled and a little embarrassed.

"Now look, we don't have much time," said Abby. "Josie, if you didn't lock Harry in Mac's room, or speak to him on the phone the other day, someone who sounds exactly like you must have done it. Who could that be?"

"I really don't know," said Josie.

"What about an impressionist?" said Harry. "Have

you ever had one on the show?"

"I don't think so," said Josie, searching her memory. "No, wait. There *was* one who auditioned. She was also a ventriloquist. Pretty good, I thought, but the judges didn't all think so, so she didn't progress in the competition."

"Have you got any footage?" said Abby.

"It didn't go out on television," said Josie. "But it'll be somewhere. Pete, can you have a search for it?"

"No problem," said a man, starting to click through files on his desktop.

"We're almost on again," said Josie, glancing at the screens. "Positions, everyone."

The next part of the show, featuring the Hot Dogs, seemed to go on for ever, but eventually there was another break.

"Found it," said Pete, calling them over.

"Well done," said Josie. "Play it on screen four."

They all crowded round. After a couple of seconds the audition footage came up. The impressionist was a sweet girl with blonde hair and glasses.

"Hello, darling," said Diamond. "Tell us about

yourself."

"My name is Lucy and I am ten years old," said Lucy confidently. "And I am the best impressionist in the world."

"Well, that is quite a statement," said Diamond, warmly. "Let's see if you're right. Good luck."

Lucy smiled and then launched into her impressions. She started with cartoon characters: Bart Simpson, SpongeBob and Droopy. Then she moved on to a famous newsreader, the prime minister, a Geordie TV presenter and a Hollywood actor.

It was impressive, but she'd saved the best for last.

"I'm now going to interview all of you," she said to the judges.

Lucy walked over to Eve. "Hello, how are you today?" she said.

Before Eve could open her mouth, Lucy started doing an impression and throwing her voice so it seemed as though Eve was speaking.

"I'm very well, thanks, and I'm really enjoying your impressions, they're great," said Lucy in Eve's voice.

Diamond was next.

"What do you think the weather will be like tomorrow?" said Lucy.

As Diamond was a singer, Lucy made her sing the answer.

"I think it might be cloudy," Lucy sang in Diamond's voice. "With sunny periods."

She moved on to Clive.

"You're a comedian, aren't you, Clive?" Lucy asked.

"Yes, I am the funny one," said Lucy, impersonating Clive speaking robotically in a very serious voice.

Finally, Lucy sidled up to Wally.

"Can I have one million pounds, please?" she said.

"Of course," said Lucy as Wally. "In fact, I'll give you ten million pounds."

The judges laughed as Lucy moved back to the centre of the room and ended with an impression of Mac.

"Thank you for watching *Britain's Biggest New Star*, goodnight."

As Josie had said, it really was pretty good. Wally and Diamond clearly thought so as well. They were up on their feet applauding, but Clive and Eve stayed sitting. They seemed less impressed and, when it came to the judging, both of them felt that Lucy was not quite ready for the live shows yet. They both gave her a no, which meant she didn't go through.

"That's weird," said Harry. "She's really good."

"You know," said Abby, "there's something about Lucy that's bothering me."

"Me too," said Harry. "She seems very familiar."

Then a voice that was also very familiar said:

"It's Rosy."

CHAPTER 30

Access All Areas

Everyone jumped.

"That's Mac," whispered Abby.

She was right. Mac had been listening in on everything through his earpiece.

"Rosy?!" said Harry and eight other people.

"As you've just seen, she's pretty good at impressions," said Mac through his microphone. "But when she told me she wanted to audition for the show, I said I didn't think it was a good idea, what with her being my niece. If she got through, people would think it was favouritism."

"But she did audition," said Harry.

"Yes," continued Mac. "She was very insistent. She said she could disguise herself so that no one would know who she was, But I knew it would come out eventually. That's why I agreed, but arranged for Clive and Eve to turn her down."

"Wow," said Abby. "But Rosy wouldn't have known that."

"Not at first," said Mac. "She was pretty angry not to get through. But then, erm, well, she borrowed my phone to play a game and saw some messages I'd sent to Clive and Eve. I can't believe she'd have anything to do with all this, though. She's so shy and sweet. . ."

"Wait," breathed Harry. "It was *her* outside Mac's dressing room. And she was pretending to be Josie when I called. She must have another phone. That's why you didn't have a clue what I was on about, Josie."

"And she was on her own in Mac's dressing room during the first show," said Abby. "She could have taken a walkie-talkie and given all those instructions pretending to be you, Josie."

"And she could have snuck into Eve's dressing room to write on the mirror. I'm also guessing she only pretended to be scared of snakes, so we'd think she was just a nervous little girl. But what about the Greta video?" said Harry.

"Ah well," said Mac sadly. "A few weeks back I had a meeting at Clive's house. Rosy said his house had been on one of those Homes of the Stars shows and she really wanted to see it. So I brought her along. I'm guessing that's when she filmed Greta and dubbed the voice on later."

"'The letters were sent from Romania," said Abby. "Mac, was Romania on your sister and her husband's route round the world?"

"It was, yes," said Mac.

"She got them to post the letters from there," said Abby. "Wow, she's put a lot of thought and planning into this."

"But when did she hypnotize you, Abby?" said Harry.

"Yes," said Josie. "She's not a hypnotist."

"Well," interjected Erran sheepishly. "She did ask me a lot of questions about hypnotism and I may have directed her to a short online course about it."

"That sounds like Rosy," said Mac over the intercom. "Once she gets her teeth into something, she goes for it."

"When did she do it, though?" said Harry. "We've been together all this time."

"Hang on," said Abby. "Harry, show me that film of Dad you took for Trevor."

Harry scrolled through his phone till he found the clip and handed it to Abby.

"There. Look. In the background," said Abby. "It's me and Rosy." She held up the phone. "We'd been looking for Tanya; she must have hypnotized me then."

Everyone watched as, on the screen, Rosy clicked her fingers and a dazed-looking Abby blinked.

"She's bringing you out of the trance," said Erran.

"This is very interesting, but you have to act now," said Mum.

They all turned to look at her. She gave a wry smile.

"I have a little insight into how criminals work," she said. "At the moment Rosy doesn't know we're on to her, which gives us an advantage. But it also means she'll go ahead and do whatever it is she's planning."

"Which is to make the show and the prince a laughing stock," said Abby slowly.

"OK," said Josie, springing into action. "There's one more part before the prince comes out, which doesn't give us long. I'll tell security to search the building for her. And, as you two are secret service agents, I suggest you do the same. Here."

She held out two passes with the letters AAA on them. Access All Areas.

"On it," said Harry proudly.

"Right, we're coming back from the break," said Josie. "Mac, keep it cool and relaxed."

With their passes dangling from their necks, Abby and Harry began a rapid search of the building.

They raced up to Mac's dressing room and started there. Rosy was pretty small, so they checked every cupboard and under every table.

"Nothing," panted Harry. "Let's go back to the ground floor."

"She could be disguised again, remember," said Abby as they charged down the stairs. "We don't know who we're looking for."

"Ugh," said Harry. "Let's split up – we'll be faster that way."

"Gotcha," said Abby. "I'll take the canteen, you do the technical area."

With her pass, Abby was also able to go in to the canteen kitchen. To the bemusement of the catering staff, she hared around opening cupboards, drawers, fridges and even oven doors.

In the technical area Harry was finding that all the equipment made it difficult to get around. There was also the fact that the show was on and a lot of people were trying to do their jobs. After searching for Rosy as best he could, he gave up and returned to the gallery just as Abby was arriving.

Mum was also there. She was sipping mint tea and looked annoyingly relaxed. On the screens the acrobatic trio were finishing their performance. Then Mac opened the vote and said that the winner would be announced after the break. They had no time to lose.

"Any luck?" Mum asked breezily.

"No," said Harry. "She's vanished and we haven't got much time left."

Mum took another sip of tea. "You know," she said, "villains usually make one stupid mistake."

"What do you mean?" said Harry.

"I'm not sure," said Mum, infuriatingly. "You'll have to work it out."

"Thanks," said Abby.

Harry and Abby racked their brains for something, anything that could lead them to Rosy. What could she have overlooked?

"Back from the break in thirty seconds," said Josie.

"Wait a minute," said Abby suddenly. "That phone number she gave you, Harry, the one that was meant to be Josie's. It'll be on your phone."

"Yes, but my phone is dead. . ."

"Plug it in here," said Abby, pointing to a socket and handing him a charger.

Harry grabbed the wire and plugged it in.

"It's turning on," he said, relieved. "And I've got the number."

"Josie," said Abby. "Can we get a camera to focus on the audience?"

Josie spoke to one of the camera operators through

her microphone. A moment later a shot of the audience appeared on one of the screens in the gallery.

"OK, Harry," said Abby. "Ring that number."

Harry pressed the call button.

"It's ringing," he said.

The twins focused in on the screen, their eyes darting this way and that.

"There!" shouted Abby. "In the mosh pit on the right."

It had been small, but someone in the crowd had their head bowed as they fumbled with a phone.

The camera zoomed in. It was a girl with red hair wearing dungarees, a scarf and tinted glasses. It was a great disguise, but up close there was no getting away from it. It was Rosy.

"We've found her!" shouted Abby. "Let's get in there and stop her!"

"It's too late," said Josie helplessly, pointing to another screen.

"What?" shrieked Harry.

"The prince is already onstage."

CHAPTER 31
The Big Moment

"Keep that camera on Rosy," shouted Abby as all the other screens showed the audience standing and His Royal Highness walking out to a fanfare of trumpets.

The finalists were lined up onstage, and glancing up, Harry could see Gus. He looked miserable. *If only he knew what was going on*, thought Harry.

"Mac, we've found Rosy," said Josie into her mike. "Keep your wits about you."

On a screen they saw Mac give a thumbs up, and then he was back in presenter mode.

"Welcome, Your Highness," he said, bowing his head. "I believe you have a few words you would like to say."

"Thank you, Mr Tatum," said the prince. He was standing at a podium in the centre of the stage. "It is a great pleasure for me to be here with you this evening..."

"Look," hissed Harry. "Rosy's taking something out of her pocket."

"Oh my goodness," cried Josie. "It's not a..."

"No," said Harry. "It's a microphone."

"That's it," gasped Abby. "She's going to throw her voice and make the prince say something terrible."

"What do we do?" said Harry.

"Leave it to me," said Josie. She pressed a button on the console in front of her and spoke into the mike.

"Sound," she said. "When I tell you, cut off the prince's microphone."

"What?" said the sound technician. "But a few moments ago you said to cut off *Mac's* microphone."

"No, I didn't," said Josie. "What are you talking about?"

"Rosy must have done it!" cried Abby. "The prince isn't her target – it's Mac. Revenge for scuppering her chances on the show."

"So what do we do?" said Harry.

"Josie," said Abby, thinking fast. "Is it possible to

divert Mac's microphone so that it is only heard in here? By us?"

"Sound?" said Josie.

"Yes, I think so, but it'll take a few moments," said the sound technician.

"OK," said Abby. "Get on to it now, but don't do it until I tell you."

Back onstage, the prince was wrapping up his speech and was now ready to announce the winner.

"I am delighted to announce," said the prince, "that the winner of *Britain's Biggest New Star* is. . ."

He paused. Being a fan of the show himself, he knew how to increase the drama. In fact, he would have made a great host himself if he hadn't been the prince.

". . .the Hot Dogs!"

The heavens opened and a shower of gold and silver confetti flooded the stage. The audience erupted and the Hot Dogs' Roisin picked up the nearest dog and hugged the life out of it, while the seven others yapped away excitedly.

Abby didn't take her eyes off Rosy for a moment.

"What about that?" said Mac. "Every dog has his

day, and this is definitely it for Hot Dogs!"

He was walking across the stage as he said it, microphone in hand. He ushered Roisin forward to join him and the prince by the podium.

"Are you ready?" said Abby.

"Nearly, nearly, I'm working as fast as I can," said the sound technician.

"Roisin, congratulations," said Mac. "What have you got to say?"

"I'm just overwhelmed, it's amazing," said Roisin. "Thank you to everyone who voted for us, I'm so grateful."

"And Your Highness," said Mac. "On behalf of

everyone here at *BBNS*, can I just say..."

"Now!" screamed Abby.

At that exact moment on a screen in the gallery, Rosy said,

"...I hate you. You stink of corgi poo and have a face like a slapped walrus."

Abby, Harry and everyone else turned back to look at the screen showing the stage.

Mac was a little bewildered and everyone else was looking at him and waiting.

"Switch Mac's mike back on," shouted Abby.

"Ah, apologies, Your Highness," said Mac onstage. "Small technical hitch. I just wanted to say, on behalf of everyone, what an honour it is for us to have you here."

Abby and Harry breathed a huge sigh of relief. No one outside of the gallery had heard what Rosy had said.

"Look," said Abby, pointing.

The camera was still on Rosy, whose face was an expression of utter horror.

"She's making a run for it!" shouted Harry.

In the mosh pit, Rosy barged past the other people and sped down the aisle; but the royal security team had now been alerted and nothing got past them. They grabbed her long before she got to the exit.

"Well done, Mac," said Josie. "Brilliant show. I'll be down in five."

She turned to the twins. "Great work, you two," she said.

They walked out of the gallery feeling relieved, but very tired. Mum was there, leaning against a wall, eating a banana.

"Where'd you get that?" said Harry,

"Mac's dressing room," Mum said. She held open her backpack. "He won't miss it. Or these grapes, oranges, crisps and chocolates."

Her bag was full to overflowing with goodies. Harry and Abby couldn't help but laugh.

"What's so funny?" said a voice behind them.

It was Gus.

"Oh, nothing," said Abby. "Sorry you didn't win, Dad."

"Beaten by dogs in suits, that's showbiz," he said with a grin on his face. "Hello, Samantha darling. Shouldn't you be getting back to your cell?"

"No rush," said Samantha. "There's a soap opera on now that everyone loves, so they won't miss me."

"Actually, Mum," said Abby, "I think we might be seeing a lot more of you in the future."

"Really," said Samantha. "What gives you that idea?"

"Just a hunch, but I think someone we know might do us a little favour now," said Abby, smiling.

"There they are, there they are," boomed a voice coming towards them. It was Mac. "The greatest secret service undercover agents on the planet!"

"What are you talking about, Mac?" said Gus.

"Don't worry, Dad," said Harry. "We'll explain later."

"I'm, ah, sorry about Rosy," said Mac to the twins. "Even though she's a distant relative of mine, I'm not going to make excuses for her behaviour. What she did was very wrong, and I salute the two of you. Well done, Henry and Abby. Now, how about we all go to the after-show party?"

"Thanks, Mac," said Gus. "But I'm afraid we've got to rush off now. There is one thing we wanted to tell you, though. . ."

"Yes?" said Mac.

Gus looked at his family and all together they shouted,

"*It's Harry!*"

CHAPTER 32
Opportunity Knocks

"*What* did you just say, Mum?" said Harry.

"I said, I've decided to enter the next series of *BBNS* as an escapologist." Samantha smiled sunnily at her children. "I've obviously got a real talent for it."

Harry shook his head in disbelief.

"I think it's a great idea, Mum," said Abby. "And with Dad as the new co-host, you can't lose."

Gus smiled from behind a newspaper he was pretending to read.

"No no," he said. "I have to be completely fair. I'm not just going to show favouritism to family members.

I'll have to show it to friends, acquaintances and people I've never met before as well."

A *lot* had happened since the final.

A couple of days after it had finished, Samantha had been told she was going to be released. Somehow, Trevor had found time in his busy schedule to pull a few strings. It had been planned for the Friday of that week, but she had escaped and returned home on the Thursday. Everyone was delighted to see her, but it did rather ruin the big welcome-home party that had been planned.

As it was, they were able to celebrate Gus's new job instead. Josie had rung to say that they'd like him to be Mac's co-host on the next series.

Apparently ratings for the show had been at an all-time high and feedback was that viewers particularly loved the way Gus and Mac interacted onstage. In particular people loved it when Gus took the mickey out of Mac.

Josie also explained that Gus had got to the final entirely on merit, there had been no secret service "intervention". If he hadn't made it through, they planned to invite all the losing semi-finalists back to watch the show from the audience. That way Gus could still have attended the final.

And there was other news as well. Aditi and Erran had been offered a show together in Las Vegas, which meant that after two days working for Clive again, Aditi had resigned and headed off to America. Greta was gutted.

Debbie and Tanya were released with a caution, but Debbie's show had suffered a huge dip in ratings. She could now no longer afford a studio, so she was recording it in her shed.

Debbie couldn't pay any staff either, so there was no job for Tanya, who was currently working in a pet shop cleaning poo out of the hamster cages.

Lady Monica Van Smedling Von Hockendoch had been stripped of her title, so was now just Monica Van Smedling Von Hockendoch. Her family were still very wealthy though, so she'd recorded an album herself called *Hockendoch Sings The Hits*. It was currently at number 11,809 in the charts.

Harry and Abby were naturally delighted to have

Mum home, *and* for Dad to be back on telly again, but apart from a couple of letters of thanks (one from the show and one from the prince), their lives were back to normal now, which meant school, school and more school.

It didn't help that a little while ago they'd been undercover agents trying to crack the biggest case in the country. The contrast made their everyday lives seem not just humdrum, but HUMDRUM!

"Hey, Abby," said Harry after a particularly dull day at school. "How about you shut your eyes and let me direct you home?"

"No thanks," said Abby. "How about *you* shut your eyes and I direct you into the nearest lamp post?"

Harry was finding life so boring that he was actually considering saying yes to this offer, when they heard a familiar voice behind them.

"What's the weather like in Madrid?"

They swung round to see Agent 4905-3, aka Trevor, standing there. He was wearing reflector sunglasses and a really sharp suit. He looked much slicker and more spy-like than he had before.

"Hang on," said Harry. "Um. It is not raining in Madrid."

"Oh, there's no need for that," said Trevor. "I'm not really here for business."

"Then why did you ask what the weather was like in Madrid?" said Abby.

"Because I might go there this weekend," said Trevor. "Anyway, I wanted to say well done to both of you on the case. I may have done the groundwork for you, but you did a very good job solving the rest of it."

Harry and Abby gave each other a look that said *yeah, right*.

"One thing's been puzzling me, though," continued Trevor. "The spanner. How did Rosy manage that? Was – was that really the curse?"

"Well," said Abby. "Either it *was* the curse. . ."

Trevor nodded earnestly.

"Or," went on Abby, "it was a genuine accident, but one that worked pretty well in Rosy's favour."

"There are no accidents in this game," said Trevor wisely. "It was definitely the curse."

"Well, you know best," said Harry faux-earnestly.

"Quite," said Trevor. "Now, first things first. Do you think you could get me a ticket to the show, now that Gus is hosting?"

"We'll see what we can do," said Abby, smiling and shaking her head. "Was there a second thing second?"

"There was," said Trevor. "Obviously our little secret has come out. My bosses weren't as angry as I thought they would be. In fact, I received a promotion for the initiative I showed in getting you two to be the undercover agents."

"How wonderful for you," said Abby sarcastically.

"Yes, but the department also feels that you two showed great intelligence and aptitude," Trevor said. "And courage under pressure."

"Go on," said Harry.

"I will," said Trevor. "It seems there are quite a lot of young criminals in the world. There was an eight-year-old in Bulgaria who wrote a guidebook that gave tourists all the wrong translations. When they thought they were asking for directions to a museum, they were in fact asking for a plate of bogies and armpit hair.

Terrible business. There was a six-year-old in Australia who put laxative into apples. That got very messy, I can tell you."

"This is fascinating, Trevor," said Abby gently. "But what has it got to do with us?"

"Well, we're setting up a new department, the CCCCCCCCC, or Centrally Coordinated Children's Criminal Centre Concentrating on Catching Child Criminals. Anyway, my promotion was to head up that department, and as such, I wondered whether you two would like to be my first recruits."

For a moment the twins thought they might be dreaming. Then they thought Trevor must be joking (although as it was Trevor, they quickly dismissed that).

"Well, what do you say?" said Trevor.

Harry and Abby looked at each other, and knew exactly what they were both going to say. Which was...

"Yes, please."

In truth, they had no idea quite what it was they had just said yes to. But they both knew one thing. Young criminals anywhere on the planet needed to be on the lookout now, because Harry and Abby were on their case – and together, there was no crime they couldn't solve.

ACKNOWLEDGEMENTS

So, acknowledgements, that's a big word. I barely know what it means. OK, OK, I do. It's basically giving a shout out to all the people who helped make this book a reality. It's saying thank you to everyone who gave me advice, suggestions, thoughts, inspiration, made me tea when I had a headache from staring at my computer for too long, did the editing of the book, the layout, the font, the pictures, negotiated my deal (yes, I actually get paid for writing this) and everyone who read it. And that's where I'm going to start. Thanks to you for reading this book because that's why writers write, so that readers can read, it really does make it worthwhile.

Thanks to all the people at the publishers, Scholastic, for all the time and effort they put in to it, and that means Genevieve, Linas, Lauren, Peter and Samantha. Thanks also to James Lancett for his cracking illustrations, I really can't draw for toffee, and am in awe of his talent.

Thanks to Ivan Mulcahy and Sallyanne Sweeney, my agents, which doesn't mean estate agents or travel agents, it means literary agents. They take care of all the business-y stuff associated with writing a book, and other things as well, like telling me I can write a little bit when I'm doubting myself.

Then there's that other part of my writing career where I have been lucky enough to work on a number of television talent shows. I have many chums from that world and I'd like to thank them for providing plenty of experiences, experiences which may have provided inspiration for parts of this book ... though, as it says as the start, any resemblance to anyone is purely coincidental.

And finally there's the fam ... Sophie, Ruby and Art ... me missus, me daughter and me son. And yes,

I know that's not proper English, but that's who they are and I love them with every part of my being, and that includes my bum.